D0771354

BUCKSHOT

A NED CODY NOVEL

BUCKSHOT

L. J. MARTIN

THORNDIKE PRESS
A part of Gale, Cengage Learning

 GALE
CENGAGE Learning·

Farmington Hills, Mich • San Francisco • New York • Waterville, Maine
Meriden, Conn • Mason, Ohio • Chicago

Copyright © 2013 by L. J. Martin.
A Ned Cody Novel.
Buckshot was originally published by Kensington Publishing as *TenKiller*.
Thorndike Press, a part of Gale, Cengage Learning.

LIBRARY OF CONGRESS CIP DATA ON FILE.
CATALOGUING IN PUBLICATION FOR THIS BOOK
IS AVAILABLE FROM THE LIBRARY OF CONGRESS

ISBN-13: 978-1-4328-3833-1 (hardcover)
ISBN-10: 1-4328-3833-4 (hardcover)

Published in 2017 by arrangement with L. J. Martin

Printed in Mexico
1 2 3 4 5 6 7 21 20 19 18 17

BUCKSHOT

CHAPTER ONE

Johnny Tenkiller got his name in the usual way, from his father. What was unusual was how seriously he took it. Talk was he'd killed ten men by the time he was twenty-one. But he must have lost count — he was still killing men, and women.

He'd pushed the little dun horse he rode to near exhaustion. Sitting quietly in the shadows of a scrub oak thicket, he watched a farmhouse. Even though only twenty feet inside the scraggly growth, he knew he couldn't be seen in the deep shadows by the man who worked in the farmyard. Johnny's dirty canvas breeches and frayed doeskin shirt melded into the dry June undergrowth. The rusted metal on the lathered mare's tack caught no reflection from the afternoon sun.

Tenkiller sat motionless. His long stringy black hair and dusty pocked complexion disappeared into the shadows. Even his cold black eyes caught no glint of light. He kept them half closed as he'd learned to do as a boy, hunting in the Chiricahua Desert in southern Arizona. His floppy-brimmed hat hung low over searching eyes, shading his face.

The farmhouse nestled in the shallow draw just a little south of Porterville, at the western foot of California's Sierra Nevadas — only forty miles north of Johnny's destination. The farm wasn't much, but the big buckskin gelding in the corral looked like a lot of horse. Spotting the buckskin from the wagon road a quarter mile away, Johnny had carefully, quietly, worked his way down through the shadows.

Three years back, after escaping Yuma prison, he'd run a buckskin horse to death in the desert just south of Sedona. And that horse had taken a lot of killing. Johnny hoped the gelding had gone to a place of green meadows and cool waters. He'd been partial to buckskins ever since.

The farmer slung slop to his hogs. Turning and walking to a water trough, he splashed some out to clean off his boots. The buckskin trotted to the corral fence nearest the oak thicket, neighing shrilly to the mare. The farmer stopped, looked at the buckskin, then at the thicket. Johnny froze, relaxing only as the man returned to his cleaning.

Tenkiller dismounted, keeping his eyes always on the working farmer, and tied the mare to an oak. Leaving his Henry rifle in its saddle scabbard — its brass receiver might catch the sun's light — he unstrapped his belt and removed his holster. Slipping the stubby Garland & Sommerville .450 revolver out of its holster, Johnny shoved it under his belt at the small of his back, his loose shirt covering it. He slipped his Bowie knife under the shirt and belt in the front. Both waited, well concealed.

The cool iron of the revolver felt good in his hand. If Johnny loved anything, since he'd left the Arizona desert, he loved that gun. He'd taken it off the body of a man who'd not been careful enough to watch the shadows of the rocks as he rode through a Utah Territory pass. Johnny's knife had been quiet and true. The traveler was a white man, and Johnny had come to know one certainty — all white men were enemies.

When he'd first inspected the action of the stubby revolver, it surprised him so much he'd dropped it. It was a self-extracting model, the spent shell casings ejected with a snap from its six-shot cylinder. That, and the big man-stopping shells it fired from its stubby frame, made it Johnny's favorite. It was a gun for close work.

The empty pail swinging from his hand, the farmer walked into the barn. Tenkiller took the opportunity to pad quietly from the scrub oak to the barn door. He stepped inside. The man worked at a small haystack in the far corner of the barn, pitchfork in hand. He turned as the door squeaked.

"Howdy," the man spoke, holding the pitchfork in both hands in front of him. It was a new fork and one he was very proud of. Store-bought, it had iron tines. Johnny had learned to respect the white man's iron when General George Crook led a troop through his village a few years before. Many Apache had felt the iron.

The farmer furrowed his graying brows and watched Tenkiller closely. It was not customary to walk up on a man anywhere in the West without calling out. Any man who failed to make his presence known was suspect. The farmer gave Johnny the once-over. Seeing no weapons, he slowly lowered the pitchfork.

"Got any water?" Tenkiller asked with his chin tucked close to his chest, habitually hiding the throat scar he carried from a lynch rope. Johnny hadn't expected a weapon of any kind and the long sharp fork surprised him. He raised his left hand palm outward in a sign of supplication and peace as he spoke.

The man motioned to the side of the barn. "Didn't you see the well? T'wixt here and the house?"

Johnny would have liked to have used his knife, but not at this distance. As he spoke, Tenkiller's right hand snaked behind his back under the shirt, slipping the revolver from his belt. He leveled the gun at the man and fired in one fluid motion. The reverberating roar of the shot shook the barn, as the barrel-chested man was flung backwards by the force of the lead slug smashing through bone.

But Henry Pickett was a man of the West. He'd come to California from Nebraska, across the Great Plains, rugged mountains, and killing deserts. Like John Tenkiller, he'd faced cold steel and the fury of battle, only his test of fire had been in Cicero, Illinois, dressed in the blue of the Union Army against the gray of the South, then again against the Sioux on the trip across the plains. Like most men who'd made those journeys, he'd take some killing.

Johnny's shot smacked dead true and knocked Pickett back against a stall fence rail. A red stain immediately soaked Pickett's chest, but he came off the rail in a bounce and flung the pitchfork underhanded. Johnny sprang backwards and to the side in one swift motion. He thought he'd been struck as the tines of the fork slammed into the closed barn door, pinning his trouser leg.

With a desperate effort, Pickett lunged forward, blood gushing from his mouth and nose. Johnny snapped off another shot, slamming him backwards again. The stall rails weren't there to stop him this time and the slug drove him to the dirt.

Still Pickett was not finished. He rolled, trying to rise. Tenkiller took a careful bead and shot him in the head. Pickett jerked spasmodically, then stilled.

"Damn," Johnny mumbled, reaching down and wrenching the fork loose. "Wasted two shells."

Johnny spun as the door slammed and a woman cried out, "Henry!"

Her footsteps, running approached the barn door. Johnny stepped back to avoid the door's swing.

"Henry . . . what?"

She stepped inside, stopping short, bringing a white-knuckled fist to her mouth when she saw her husband in a rapidly spreading pool of blood on the barn floor.

"Oh . . . Hen—"

She didn't have the opportunity to finish her desperate cry as Tenkiller brought the stubby, heavy revolver down across her head. She was out cold as the half-breed rolled her to her back. He set the revolver aside only long enough to throw her skirt up. He didn't bother to remove the cotton drawers that covered her from waist to knees. It took both hands to rip the well-sewn crotch open. He dropped his pants, then returned the gun to his hand as he pleasured himself.

To his surprise she was almost good-looking, not that it mattered much. The soft white skin of her lower belly excited him. It had been weeks since he'd taken a woman. The rape of a conquered enemy — not a crime to an Apache — was a right of conquest.

She awoke, saw the pockmarked face of the half-breed distorted in pleasure over her, and screamed. Johnny smashed her with the heavy revolver, again and again. She would be pretty no more but it didn't matter. She'd joined her husband.

Johnny hitched up his pants and padded to the house. Alert for others about the farm, he entered quietly. The door slammed behind him, surprising him. Springing aside, he spun, crouching and drawing his revolver in an easy motion, but holstered the weapon when he saw the farmer had rigged a counterweight to keep the door closed and the flies out of his wife's kitchen.

Two framed silhouettes of children on the kitchen wall over the table stared in reproachful silence. Had it been an earlier time, and had it been the Arizona desert, Johnny would have waited and taken the children captive, raising them in a manner he felt far superior to what he'd witnessed in his travels among the white men.

On each side of the silhouettes hung samplers. Johnny could barely read, but he was in no hurry. The subjects of the silhouettes must be at the white man's school. He ran his hands across the raised stitches of a cotton sampler . . . Home . . . Sweet . . . Home. He walked around the table and repeated the process. Peace . . . On . . . Earth. Both were subjects he had little knowledge of, at least in the last few years.

He quickly filled a flour sack with food from the cooler cabinet, then went to another upright cabinet. Johnny didn't know a pie safe from a sideboard but he recognized its contents. Removing the tin pan, he sat at the table, enjoying half of the

14

last peach pie the woman would ever bake.

By the time the children walked the five miles home from school, Johnny was well into the mountains astride Pickett's buckskin gelding. He drove the strong horse relentlessly on toward Bakersfield.

The children enjoyed a piece of the pie their mother must have left out for them before they went outside looking for her.

CHAPTER TWO

Bakersfield City Marshal Ned Cody sat in the newfangled oak swivel-back chair, his long legs perched on the edge of his oak desk, and read the telegram from Sheriff Henry S. Potter.

> Sheriff Howard/Marshal Coty
> John Tenkiller said to be heading
> your way stop last seen riding
> bay with three white stockings
> stop known to have killed
> six men our county stop please
> detain stop I will arrive 7/08/1878
> stop
> Henry S. Potter
> Sheriff,
> Laramie, Wyoming

Ned was only slightly miffed that the Wyoming sheriff had misspelled his name. At least the boy from the telegraph office delivered it to him first — that was some consolation. Of course, his office was only a block away from the telegraph and freight office. George Howard, the Sheriff, was the county law but acted as if he ran the city too, and that had already caused conflict between the two jurisdictions.

Dropping his booted feet to the pine floor, Cody rose and pulled a wide-brimmed hat tightly onto his full head of dark hair, then ambled to the inner door. He had to duck slightly as his tall frame wouldn't clear with the hat on.

"Theodore," Ned yelled to his deputy, who was supposed to be cleaning the two small cells in the back of the Marshall's office. "I've got to go to Howard's office." Getting no answer, he yelled again. "Hey, Ratzlaff!" Ned walked into the back room. Both cell doors were standing wide open, not that it mattered much. Their only occupant was sleeping off a three-day drunk. The door into the courtroom, which doubled as the town meeting hall, stood ajar.

Ned poked his head through and, as he suspected, Theodore leaned on his mop making eyes at the pretty little Mexican girl who was on her hands and knees, busily scrubbing sticky beer stains from the pine flooring, in preparation for the Sunday services the Baptists would hold the next morning. Ned focused deep brown eyes on his brawny door-filling-big deputy. "Deputy Ratzlaff, could I trouble you to watch the shop while I go over to the Sheriff's office?"

Ratzlaff looked up, irritated at being interrupted. He swept his tawny hair out of his eyes with a huge freckled hand and replied, "Sure. You gonna' be long? I gotta make my rounds soon as I finish this moppin'."

The Mexican looked up from her work and batted her long eyelashes. "Good morning, Marshall Cody."

"Mornin'." Ned smiled, then turned his attention back to Theo. "I'll make 'em. You stick close to the desk." Ned spun on his heel and made for the door. He slowed only long enough to grab the big Colt .44 that hung from a coat tree, strapping it on his waist as he strode out and across the board front step.

Theodore was a good deputy, Ned thought. Big and strong, slow and steady, he backed you with authority. His freckled face and overgrown boyish looks had fooled many a man. But Theo still hadn't gotten over being passed over for the Marshal's job. He'd been a deputy five years before Ned was hired, but when Marshal Hiram H. Nelson had been smashed up in a wagon wreck, it was Ned that he'd recommended for his job.

Ned had only worked as a deputy for Hiram a little over a year. No one was more surprised than Ned himself when Hiram stood up for him. Hiram had worked the Wells Fargo stage as a guard with Ned's father and that's what most of the town figured was his reason. But most of the town also figured that it wasn't a very good reason. Ned had had too little experience. But Hiram had talked long and hard. "He's big enough, smart enough, and damn sure tough enough," Hiram had said to the City Council, "and he's got even more grit than his father had." Ned had been surprised that Hiram had added the bit about grit. To hear Hiram tell it, no man had ever had more gumption nor pure "abide-by-the-law cussedness" than Byron T. Cody, Ned's father.

The street bustled with wagons and men on horseback. Miners, drovers, Chinese railroad workers, Mexican *vaqueros,* and an occasional townsman in a derby hat moved and threaded their way about their business. They shouted at each other and cussed their stock, as wagons and horses clattered, clanged, and squeaked along. Every day the town grew larger.

Bakersfield had recently become the Kern

County seat and Sheriff George Howard's office was a few blocks away in the newly constructed courthouse.

Ned mopped his brow with a kerchief. It was already Hades hot. He made his way east on Seventeenth Street to Chester, the town's wide main street. It was a mess. Harold "Nels" Nelson, one of the town's leading citizens and the Chairman of the City Council, was building a newfangled transportation system. He called them streetcars. The road was torn up. Dust billowed and iron rang on iron as workmen installed rails for the horse-drawn cars to run on. It was rumored that they would haul twelve passengers at one time.

Cody waved at a passing drover and tipped his hat to the preacher's wife, whose prune-like face lit up in response to the handsome young man's courtesy.

The streetcars would not have been practical if it hadn't been for the railroad. When they'd wanted to run their line through Bakersfield, the city fathers would not grant them the two blocks on each side of the tracks that the railroad insisted upon. The council said one block on each side was enough. Southern Pacific, in their tried-and-true independent manner, said fine, we'll build our own town . . . and did. Sumner

20

was built on the east side of Bakersfield, a little over a mile away.

Now freight and people moved back and forth several times a day from Sumner to Bakersfield, and the streetcars seemed a practical solution.

And Nels Nelson was just the man to make it happen, and to profit from it.

Nelson stood, with his hands on hips, watching the workers' progress. Even in the sweltering heat, he wore a split-tailed coat and cravat. He glared as Ned walked up. Nelson's fair complexion was a little redder than usual due to the heat and his dogged determination to stand out in it and see that the work went his way. "You'd be better off if you didn't wear that horse pistol when you're making your rounds, Marshal. We're trying to let people know this is a peaceful town." Nelson had been one of two dissenting votes when Ned was appointed Marshal.

Ned bit his tongue and did not reply. He looked down at the shorter man, removed his hat, and mopped his brow with his bandanna. "Sometimes I do, sometimes I don't. Seems to me folks want to see their Marshal lookin' like one, least at times."

"Humph," was the best Nelson could muster. He turned his attention back to his crew. "Watch the alignment of that rail, you yellow fool." A coolie in a pointed basket-hat gave him a quick look but did not respond.

Ned made his way across the street, wishing he'd thought to show Nelson the telegram in his pocket and ask him if he wanted to take on the job of greeting the visitor mentioned. Cody didn't relish the prospect himself. But he doubted if Nelson would even stay in the county if he had to face a man like Tenkiller. Nels might be good with money, but Ned was sure he didn't have the stand-up grit his brother Hiram had.

Ned found it a real problem being respectful to Nels Nelson. If only he wasn't Hiram's brother and Mary Beth's father . . .

"Toothless," Ned yelled at a little wizened Chinaman making his way out of Callahan's Chop House. Gum San Choy had a bundle of laundry hanging from the same hand that balanced a basket full of eggs on his head. Another basket of jars hung from the other arm. Gum San smelled of tobacco, bleach, and pickling spices. His business was eggs — raw, boiled, and pickled — and laundry.

"Awww, Marsha' Ned, son of honorable friend," Toothless said, bowing his head in respect for Ned's dead father. It was a ritual that the little yellow man always followed. He raised his head and grinned, his gums rosy and barren in the bright June sun.

"I could use your help, honored friend of my father's" Ned said respectfully. Toothless smiled even broader and nodded his head, the egg basket shaking precariously and his queue dancing with the effort. Ned continued, "There's a man coming who I must find and arrest. He will be coming from the north or the east, and will be on horseback. I know little of him, except that he had taken the lives of many men and is half Mexican and half Apache." At the mention of Apache the toothless smile faded.

He should be here soon," Ned continued. "He will go into the Tenderloin. When I know more of him, I will call for you, honored friend of my father." Ned waited for an affirmative nod, then continued. "Tell your people to watch for him. And then you come to see me."

Toothless nodded gravely, the egg basket again bobbing dangerously as he did so. He turned and scuffled off down the dirt street, quilted trousers flapping and leather sandals slapping his calloused heels.

Nobody knew the Tenderloin like Toothless. Five blocks long, it began one block east of the town's main street. L Street ran north and south and was lined with saloons and gambling halls on the south end and

23

rooming houses and Chinese joss houses on the north. At sunset cribs with doors and curtained windows opening right onto the street lit up, coal-oil lights illuminating the current scantily dressed occupant plying her trade to the passersby.

Ned noticed a big bay stallion tied to the rail outside of Callahan's. The silver *conchos* on its bridle and trimming its saddle glistened in the hot sun. He knew who the horse belonged to.

Making his way into Callahan's Chop House, Ned kicked his way through sawdust and peanut shells left over from the night before. The place reeked of stale beer, tobacco, and sweaty men, but it was empty now except for the bartender and a lone figure standing at the bar.

Alvarado Cuen stood quietly, his face hidden by the full *sombrero* he wore. Al never wore a gun. His weapons were the *reata* that was tied to the saddle of the big stallion at the rail outside and a blacksnake whip. The whip's tight woven leather was looped and bound with a thong to the back of Al's tight embroidered breeches at the belt line. Ned had seen Cuen cut a cigar in half while still in a man's mouth with that long coiled leather.

Ned had never said more than ten words

to Cuen, but he respected him. Alvarado minded his own business and never caused trouble. But he never turned from it either.

It was ten in the morning. Al sipped the strong cane liquor favored by the Mexican, an *aguardiente,* strong enough to burn the hair off a hog's back. "Alvarado," Ned called as he approached.

The tall man turned and touched the brim of the big *sombrero.* "Marshal," he said, then turned back to his drink.

"You got a minute?" Ned pressed him. "You might be able to help me with a problem." Ned explained quickly that Ten-killer was said to be coming and that he would appreciate knowing of the arrival of anyone fitting his description.

Cuen looked at Ned for a long moment. Turning back to his drink he lit up a long, thin black cheroot, popping the sulfur match with his thumb nail. He inhaled deeply, then dropped the played-out match to the floor. Exhaling, he spoke quietly. "I have not had help from you or any badge, nor any *gringo.* Why should I be of help? Especially when you say this man is half Mexican." Al drained his drink, wiping his mouth with the back of a bronzed, calloused hand. "He is the blood of my blood."

"He has the blood of many men on his

25

hands. Some of them may have been 'the blood of your blood'."

Cuen looked at Ned with cold black eyes. "I think I will let the law handle it. They have been so good, and so fair, with the *campasins,* the poor *Mexicanos.*"

Ned felt the muscles tense in his arms and back. Cuen had an old, festering burr under his saddle. Ned knew how Cuen's family had been treated after California's Bear Revolution, and that treatment would have been justified almost any amount of bitterness. But Ned had not been a party to it.

A big, rawboned hand slapped a wet towel in front of Ned with a bang, giving both men an excuse to break the hard silent gaze between them. "You want a drink, Marshal?" Jimmy "One Eye" Callahan wiped the bar. His two perfectly good eyes stared at Ned, awaiting an answer. The bartender's nickname was the result of the single-shot sawed-off shotgun he kept under the bar. Whenever a patron would get a mite out of hand, Callahan was known to whip out the "peacemaker" and inform the rowdy customer, "Ol' Bessie's one eye will see you to the door."

"No thanks, Callahan. I was just lookin' for a little help from *Señor* Cuen." Ned turned and made his way out of the bar.

"I'm buyin'," the big bartender called out behind him. Ned waved and looked back over his shoulder, not trusting the tall, surly Mexican.

Ned was still staring over his shoulder at the flashing black eyes of the *vaquero* when he pushed his way through the swinging doors, stumbling into someone.

"Oh, you made me drop my package," Mary Beth Nelson stammered.

Her pale blue eyes were framed with golden curls. Her pert nose wrinkled. Mary Beth was the only girl in town that had turned Cody's head. Ned wanted to ask her father if he could call on her, but he had never been able to bring himself to ask anything of Nels Nelson.

"I'm sorry Mary Beth . . . Miss Nelson." Ned grabbed up the package, then tipped his hat to her. She snatched the package out of his hand.

"You look mighty pretty," Ned told her. "Feathered out like Sunday morning."

Mary Beth ignored the compliment, but fixed her cool, blue eyes on him. "It's a little early to be in the saloon, isn't it, *Marshal*?" It seemed obvious that she shared her father's feelings.

"All in the line of duty, ma'am," Ned mumbled. Mary Beth turned and made her

27

way down the boardwalk, her honey-blond hair almost reaching the bobbing bustle of the dress.

Ned adjusted his hat and the big .44 at his side as he watched the bustle wave saucily at him. Then he turned and headed for the Sheriff's office. As he walked, he wondered which were meaner than snake-bit mules. Womenfolk or *vaqueros*? Maybe both.

So far it wasn't turning out to be his best day.

CHAPTER THREE

Sheriff George Howard sat at his massive oak rolltop desk and stared out the window of his new office. He scratched his balding, liver-spotted head, then rested his hands on the broad expanse of his belly, and closed his eyes, deep in thought. In four months he would face his first re-election and he wasn't looking forward to it. He hadn't made a lot of friends among the city fathers, and the city made up almost half the votes he needed.

The good news was that he had plenty of money this time. The pimps and gamblers of Bakersfield, Sumner, and Caliente had paid well for the protection of his office.

But money might not solve all his problems. The do-gooders of the city had been raising a lot of hell about the Tenderloin and were putting a lot of pressure on the new City Marshal, Cody, to clean it up. Sheriff Howard was receiving his share of pressure about the county problems, particularly Sumner, which was less than a mile from the city limits. Just last week, *The Southern Californian,* the local weekly, had an unflattering article about the killings in a Sumner saloon. The headline had read, "Sheriff in Caliente While Killers Were Here."

Howard was sorry to see Caliente come apart at the seams. When it had been the railhead it had been a gold mine for him. Now that the rails had been pushed westward over the mountains, there wasn't much reason for the little town. Only two years ago Caliente had twenty-two saloons. Now it had two, and they weren't busy.

"Cap!" George yelled. Cap Colston stuck his round red face through the door. His unbuttoned vest hung open, a watch chain dangled from one pocket, and a miniature George Howard belly bulged against the buttons of his shirt. "You seen Winston and Puttyworth? They should have been back early."

"Not yet, Sheriff." Colston blinked small, browless eyes under a green visor. "They'll come in straightaway. They know better than to mess about."

"Bring me a cup of that mud you call coffee," the Sheriff said. "And the 'take' reports from last week."

"You got 'em in your safe, Sheriff. You tol' me plenty of times not to have them about my desk." Cap exited to the outer office.

Sheriff Howard walked over and knelt in front of the large green safe which commanded a corner of the office, his easy movement belying his size. Cap reappeared, balancing a tray rattling with a pot, cups, cream pitcher, and sugar bowl. He shoved a pile of papers out of the way and managed to set the tray on the Sheriff's cluttered desk.

The heavy door of the safe creaked open, Howard ruffled through a pile of records, rose, hustled to his desk, and sat down. Cap started to return to his desk to get back into his dime novel.

"Wait a minute, Cap. Take this mess back." Howard poured himself a half cup of the thick black coffee, spooned in two heaping spoons of sugar, then topped the cup off with cream. Cap blinked nervously as he returned to the Sheriff's desk. While Cap was clearing the tray, Howard thumbed through the black book he'd gotten from the safe. He pulled at a large, hairy earlobe with the thick fingers of one hand and complained, "If things don't get better, you boys ain't gonna' get no bonus this month."

31

Cap stopped and looked at the Sheriff over the top of his half glasses, but didn't comment. He walked out of the office and back to the novel he'd stuffed under the clutter on his desk. "Son of a bitch," he muttered quietly to himself, blinking nervously.

Cap had just settled back into his story and the exciting Indian fight when the Sheriff called again. "Watch what you got laying about. Here come Bakersfield's best."

Cap adjusted his visor and squinted as he looked through the door and out the Sheriff's window. Sheriff Howard moved with surprising speed for a fat man. Kneeling at the safe he stuffed the black book in and slammed the heavy door, stood and walked to the window.

Watching the young City Marshal make his way across Railroad Avenue toward the courthouse, the sheriff shook his head and muttered. "That old .44's got a barrel like a cannon. Hope the peckerhead never has to jerk it in a hurry." He turned to his clerk. "Then again" — Howard smiled, displaying a mouthful of yellowing teeth — "that might solve some of our problems."

The sheriff returned to his desk, sat down, propped his feet up, and waited to see what the new City Marshal had on his mind.

32

Marshal Cody opened the tall front door, admiring the scrolled "Court House" that had been etched into the center of an oval glass panel. Passing the stairway that led to the second floor of the impressive brick building, Ned opened the door at the end of the hall marked "Sheriff's Office."

Cap Colston bent over his books, busily making entries. "Cap, the Sheriff in?" Cody asked.

Colston looked up and glared at Ned, as if irritated at being interrupted. He stood and headed for the inner door. "I'll check," he said.

It irked Cody the way he was always treated at the Sheriff's office. Cap knew whether or not the Sheriff was in. The inner door was the only way out of his office. Unless he'd escaped out the window.

Cap stuck his head through the door, then turned back to Cody. "He'll be with you in a minute. Have a seat."

Cody remained standing.

Ned passed the time studying the wanted posters on the bulletin board. Finally, Cap turned from his work. "You can go in now, Marshal."

Cody wondered what secret communications systems the officious little man had with the Sheriff. Or had the Sheriff merely told him to keep Cody waiting? He shook his head and walked into the office. George Howard was leaning far back in his swivel chair, feet propped on his desk, his potbelly exposed where his shirt parted between stressed buttons. The hair on his sweaty belly was matted and just a little thinner than the hair on his head.

Howard dug a cigar out of the drawer, bit off the end, lit it, and puffed a couple of times. He spit a bit of brown, soggy leaf on the floor, then spoke. "Have a seat, Ned boy. What can we do for you?"

Cody fished the flimsy yellow telegram out of his shirt pocket and handed it to the Sheriff. "Looks like a little trouble might be headin' our way."

Howard read the telegram and flipped it casually onto the pile on his desk. "Who brought this to you?"

"The delivery boy. Why?"

"No reason. This may be more than a little trouble, Ned boy. Let me show you." He ruffled through a bottom drawer of the desk with stubby tobacco-stained fingers.

While he searched for the wanted poster, Howard made a mental note to have a talk with Pete at the telegraph office. By God, he was the Sheriff of this county, and he would not stand for getting secondhand information. Particularly not second to a pretty-boy City Marshal, even if he was Byron T. Cody's son. The Sheriff found what he was looking for and handed it to Cody. "Take a gander at this. Came through a couple of months ago."

Ned unfolded the poster and turned it over. The likeness of the man held his attention for a moment. It depicted a sallow, pockmarked, mean-eyed man with long, stringy hair. The artist had inked in the word "scar" and had an arrow pointing to his upper throat.

WANTED
Dead or Alive

Murder, Robbery, Rape
Jailbreak Yuma Prison
John Tenkiller
half-breed Mexican/Apache
tall, dark, black eyes, black hair
scar from hangman's rope on
upper throat
Henry Rifle/Navy Colt/Bowie Knife
Known to trade coats with the
Harvey gang

Henry S. Potter, Sheriff
Laramie, Wyoming

"An' that's not all." The fat Sheriff blew a smoke ring. "Heard he killed men, and women, in Utah an' Arizona, and a couple of miners up around Virginia City not more than a month ago." George Howard rose and walked to the window, the cigar clamped between his teeth, his hands folded behind his back. "This boy leaves bodies behind the spits o' chaw from a heavy chewer. You ought to leave this to me, even if he shows up in the city limits."

Ned could feel heat prickle the back of his neck. He bit back the urge to tell the fat man to sit on his thumb. "Why's that, Sheriff Howard?"

"Well, we got more men and all. And I can call in deputies from Keene, Tehachapi, and Mojave. If'n we need 'em."

"If he comes our way, and it looks like we need help, I'll yell out, Sheriff." Cody's mouth curled in a half smile. "You do the same, if he shows up in the county. We'll be glad to lend you a hand."

"Humph," the Sheriff grunted, chomping down on his cigar. As Ned headed for the door, the Sheriff added, "You an' Teddy Rat had better be real careful. This ain't no digger Indian."

Ned cringed. Theodore Ratzlaff hated only one thing worse than being called Teddy.

That was being called Rat. Had Ned's big deputy been along there would have been a fight, and Sheriff Howard would have ended up eating his big, sloppy cigar.

"We always try to be careful, Sheriff. I'll mention that to Ratzlaff. All of it." Cody smiled. The glass rattled in the door as he slammed it behind him.

Cap jumped, blinking repeatedly. He stuffed his dime novel into a desk drawer as Cody stomped by.

"Thanks, Blinky," Ned said over his shoulder, leaving the outer door open. Colston cursed quietly under his breath as Howard yelled for him again.

Cody strode determinedly across Railroad Avenue heading for his office thinking. "Three for three. Would have been a good day to go fishin'."

CHAPTER FOUR

Tenkiller left the wagon road when he spotted the river and ferry in the distance.

The thought of paying the man to cross the quiet water galled him. He would have paid the ferryman with his knife blade, taking the money he knew the man must have, had Tenkiller not been so close to Bakersfield. But that would have to wait until Johnny was on his way out of town. It would not do to have too much trouble too soon.

Johnny sat on his haunches under a river willow watching the ferryboat unload a small band of sheep. The man tending the ferry had done his share of work, poling the ferry across the Kern River, and now he waited patiently for the clattering, baa-ing sheep to scramble off.

The thick-shouldered Basque shepherd pounded his staff on the wooden deck, hurrying the band onto the shore, where the bigger part of his trust was being guarded by two dogs. One of the spotted dogs stood perfectly still, staring at the shaded place where Johnny crouched. The dog began whimpering, then turned, and quickly gathered the sheep into a tighter circle.

Johnny knew that most men would have been looking at the sheep with the thought of mutton chops or a roast leg. But he was admiring the dog, thinking how good it would look turning over an open fire.

Tenkiller backed silently into the brush, then turned and made his way back to where he'd left the buckskin.

Working his way downstream, he looked for a fordable spot.

City Deputy Marshal Theodore Ratzlaff loped the big gelding down Chinaman's Grade to the river crossing. He decided it was too hot for him or the horse to be working so hard and slowed the gray to a walk. Reining up for a moment where the trail sloped down a big cut nestled between the town and the river, he looked out across the barren low hills, letting the gray catch his breath. The hills were golden with dry grasses, except for the occasional white slash of a water-eroded ravine. One dark spot marked a bothersome tar seep to be avoided by all but those who needed the black slime for creaking wheel hubs. Ratzlaff could see for miles to the north from this high spot.

A band of sheep grazed their way into the hills on the far side of the Kern River, away from the shade of its high cottonwoods, shorter willows, and tangled wild blackberry vines. The rough board flat-boat ferry was tied up on the near side, where the attendant's shack sat. The ferry's three-braided line spanned the river catching the occasional errant floating branch. Movement caught Theo's eye a half mile downstream from the ferry. A lone rider was crossing the river. The rider was almost a mile away. Theo wished he'd brought along the "bring 'em close," but the telescope still hung on the wall in the office.

It wasn't that unusual for a man to be fording the river, Ratzlaff thought as he studied the distant rider and his buckskin horse. The winter runoff was past. He'd forded himself when he didn't have, or didn't want to spend, the necessary dime.

Still Ratzlaff strained his eyes, shading his vision with a hamlike, freckled hand. He wished he'd passed the rider somewhere along the trail. He would have liked a much closer look. He probably should try to intercept the rider before he got to Bakersfield, but he might not be able to do so. And besides, it was just too damn hot.

As Theo reached the bottom of the grade, the trail widened onto a sandy flat. The gray plodded through the sand leading to the attendant's shack and the shade of the cottonwoods that lined the quiet river.

Old Maxwell Twill had been tending the ferry as long as Theodore could remember. Max had always had sweets — a piece of taffy or a gumdrop — for the children that rode the ferry. As a boy Theo had gotten more than his share. Max would show the boys the best places to fish and had strung a rope for them to swing on at a swimming hole near the ferry.

Theo yelled out to the old man as he reined up his horse. Twill came to the door, his shoulders slightly bent and his hands gnarled and calloused from constantly tugging hemp rope.

"Hello, Theo. You crossin'?"

"No, Max, not today. Ned asked me to come on down. Thought you might keep an eye out for a fella' we think might be headin' south."

"Well, come on in. I got a big mug of lemonade here just waitin' for the right thirst to come along."

Ratzlaff uncoiled his large frame off the gray which shook its lathered withers like a dog, before lowering his muzzle into a wooden water trough.

Shaking hands warmly with his old friend, Theo again marveled at the strength in the gnarled twisted old hands. He followed Twill into the tiny shack, plopped down at Max's table, and dug the makings out of his shirt pocket. Soon he had rolled himself and Max two misshaped cigarettes. Theo sipped the cool lemonade, visited with the old man, and smoked for half an hour before riding back to town.

All along the trail on the return trip, Theo watched for a camp where the lone rider might have stopped, but spotted nothing.

Ned Cody stood, legs apart, arms out from his sides, his long, slender fingers spread. Mentally counting to three, he grabbed, left hand across his body to the butt-forward .44. Once unholstered, the big gun roared. But his adversary — a tobacco can — sat unmoving atop the log.

Ned shook his head and, grumbling under his breath replaced the gun. The next time he pulled it, the gun bucked and the can fell forward into the dirt as the lead slug scattered splinters of the log. At least he'd hit something.

Trying to place a mental picture of the

pocked face of Tenkiller onto the tobacco can, Ned retrieved it and placed it back on the log. He retraced his twenty paces. This time he didn't try to quick-draw, but carefully laid the sights on the can, his arm fully extended. The gun belched flame and the can flew ten feet in the air.

He retrieved it again, but it was blown into such a misshaped mess it was barely a target. Ned sat on the log and pondered the fact that, as Marshal, he'd never before faced a man with a gun. He had never, in fact, even pulled a gun in the line of duty. He'd hit the tobacco can on the third careful try, but then again, it wasn't shooting back.

For the son of an old-time lawman and renowned Wells Fargo stage guard, Ned hadn't had a lot of experience with guns. His dad had always been too busy or away guarding the gold and silver shipments of the company to teach him. Byron T. Cody had been a big, quiet man, with a big reputation. Ned wondered if he'd ever be the lawman his father had been.

As a boy, Ned had spent most of his time with Mrs. McGillicutty, a buxom, rotund lady who ran the boardinghouse where Ned and his father had lived since Ned was ten. He couldn't think of her without remembering the smell of dinner rolls browning in the oven, and the big hug she had always had for him.

He and his father moved to the boardinghouse just after Ned's mother died of the fever. Mrs. McGillicutty and her husband, who ran the livery had never been blessed with children, and she more than made up for it with Ned. While Mr. McGillicutty — a New England Yankee with a thin face, hawk-beak nose, and warm, reassuring manner, who seldom said more than yep or nope — not only helped raise Ned but allowed him work in the livery to earn spending money.

When Ned was sixteen, Mrs. Mac, as he called her, died a long slow death, and Ned cried more than he had at his own mother's funeral. Mr. McGillicutty shut down the boardinghouse but offered to let Ned and his father stay on. Ned did for a few months, until his father began spending more and more time at his job — out of town and away from Ned. Then, while his father was away on another extended trip, Ned packed up and headed out.

He learned to work cattle up through the Owens Valley, on the east slope of the Sierras and into the northern Nevada territory. He learned other things too, things

44

that only a hard life among hard men can teach you. But the only gun he'd ever carried was an old, scarred, single-shot, breech-loading Springfield rifle, and it had only been fired when he needed camp meat — and one other time.

Determined to make his own way, Ned headed out of the San Joaquin Valley following the miners' trail up the Kern River through the rugged Kern Canyon to the miners' camp of Whiskey Flats. Then he followed the trail to the pass named for Joseph Reddeford Walker but used for thousands of years by Indian traders before him.

For two weeks, riding at the base of the huge granite-shouldered mountains, he'd seen no one. He killed a doe and spent three days in the bottom of a steep canyon, next to a trickling creek, resting, smoking the meat to jerky and wondering if the life of a mountain man was for him.

He traveled north for the next three days, sticking to the base of the Sierra Nevada Mountains and the long, fertile valley between them and the White Mountains farther on to the east. The Sierras rose thousands of feet above him, their sharp, rugged peaks white with snow and ice. Due east and eleven thousand feet below Mt. Whitney, the country's highest peak, Ned

45

reached Independence, the first settlement since he'd left Whiskey Flats. He was ready for other folks and home cooking.

Figuring the best place to meet people in a new town was the church or the saloon, and since it wasn't Sunday, he chose the latter. He watered, then tied his horse alongside several others, loosened the cinch, then went in.

The Revelry Saloon squatted perfectly square, a free-standing building with a wide porch the width of its front. Two Paiute Indians rested on their haunches, in long-sleeve checkered shirts and loincloths and with floppy-brimmed hats with single feathers and calf-high leggings. They eyed Ned as he entered.

It wasn't a fancy place as saloons go. The bar consisted of boards resting across two on-end hogs-head barrels. The floor might as well have been dirt as it was covered with tracked mud, straw, peanut shells, eggshells, and broken pieces of clay mugs. Smoke from store-bought cigars and hand-rolled cigarettes gathered over the bar and tables, and added an acrid odor to that of sweating, drinking patrons. Six men leaned on the boards that served as the bar, and several more sat at tables drinking, chewing, and passing playing cards and chips

46

without comment.

The place quieted as a new face appeared in the door. Ned hesitated, scanning the rough-looking hands and miners. He steeled his resolve, and strode to the bar.

"A beer please," he mumbled to a snaggle-toothed man behind the bar wearing a dingy white shirt, cravat, and garter about his upper arm. The man grabbed a clay mug, took the lid off a barrel against the wall, and dipped it full.

"Five cents." The bartender held back the mug and eyed Ned suspiciously as if he didn't have any money. Ned laid the coin on the boards, and the man set the mug down without further comment.

The other men at the bar stepped back and appraised the boy for a moment. Ned caught the look as one bushy-browed man winked to another.

The winker spoke. "I'm outta smokes, boy. Could you loan a body the fixin's?"

"Don't use tobacco," Ned answered. He noticed the drawstring from a tobacco sack hanging out of the man's shirt pocket and thought to himself that he wouldn't give the man "the fixin's" if he carried them.

"Well, how about givin' a fella a chew?" the man pressed, stepping closer to him, frowning so his bushy brows touched.

Ned stepped back. "Like I said, mister. Don't use tobacco."

"You not from around these parts, boy?"

"Name's Ned Cody, mister." Ned was eye to eye with the stranger. The man must have had thirty pounds on him. "I'm from over the mountain. Bakersfield."

"Well, it's a custom hereabouts for a new fella to stand the house to a drink." The man leaned over and spat a wad of chaw into a tarnished brass spittoon. Then he glared at Ned, wiping a dribble from his chin with the back of his hand. "You look like a man what follows a custom." The man smiled showing tobacco-stained teeth, and his friends laughed quietly.

"Might be custom 'hereabouts', but not where I come from." Ned faced back to the bar, hoping the man had finished having his fun. Ned figured the man to be well over six foot. He looked rawhide-lean and brush-busting tough. He dressed like a cowhand, except for the low-slung Colt .45 he wore and the smaller belly gun he'd stuck in his belt. He wore a skinny-brimmed bowler city hat, and a bushy, untrimmed mustache.

"Bakersfield. That's a long ride for a boy alone. You come here to chase the gold, or to teach us how to gamble?"

The other men chuckled, and Ned felt his

neck redden. He turned back to the man. "Don't know nothing about chasin' gold and less about gamblin'. I'm looking for work. Drivin' cattle or whatever."

The tall man turned to his friends. "Well, I shoulda' knowed. This here's a cattleman." Again the men chuckled.

Another group at a nearby table noticed the conversation. Ned watched as a colored man got up and walked up behind the tall fellow in the bowler.

Ned had known a couple of Blacks from Bakersfield. Both men worked as drovers alongside the Mexican *vaqueros.* They said little and come to town only on rare occasions. This man was so black he shined blue, except for a stubble of gray beard and a scar across his cheek like a slash of raw meat in a tar spill. The scar went from his forehead across his eye and down his cheek, parting the few days' growth of gray whiskers. He was a big man, not as tall as the winker that chided Ned, but wider and more powerful. He wore Cavalry pants, with a U.S.-marked, flapped holster for his dragoon Colt. Ned decided that if the mean-looking Black got into the teasing, it might be a good time to head out.

But the Black walked up behind the taller man and spoke quietly. "Since when did you

49

take up the job of welcomin' committee, Birchtold? Looks like you're doin' a miserable job of it." The big Black turned to the scraggly bartender. "Birchtold here wants to buy this fella' a beer." The Black pointed to Ned and Ned breathed a little easier. Then the Black turned and raised his face nose to nose with the taller man. "Don't ya, Birchtold." It wasn't a statement; it was a demand.

"I'm . . . I'm down to my last dollar, Henry," the tall man stammered.

"Don't take no dollar to buy a beer. In fact, I seem t' recall you owe me four bits. Pete, make that a beer an' three fingers of Who Hit John."

The tall man scowled, downed the rest of his mug of beer, and wiped the foam from his mustache with the back of his hand. He looked for a moment as if he might take a swing at the Black, then cut his eyes away and reached deep in his homespun trousers pocket. He came up with a handful of change and slapped it on the bar. The Black turned his back on the man and extended a broad, callused, pink-palmed hand to Ned.

"Name's Henry Clay Hammer. Welcome to Independence."

Ned gratefully took the hand. "I'm Ned Cody," he said, then upended his mug of

50

beer and set the empty next to the full one the bartender had provided. He put a hand over his mouth and belched, unaccustomed to the drink. "I thank you . . . an' the welcomin' committee for the beer."

The tall man the Black had called Birchtold mumbled under his breath. "Smart-ass pilgrim pup." He turned from the bar, walked to a table, and joined a poker game.

"Heard you say you was lookin' for work, Ned Cody. You a fair hand?" The scar on the Black's eye danced, as he looked from side to side.

It made Ned a little self-conscious. He had trouble looking the big man square in the eye as he answered, "I've handled my share of horses . . . trained and broke . . . but I never worked cattle. I learn quick, though. I'd work for half wages till I learned."

"I'll tell you, boy. Half a hand's wages in these parts won't buy boot leather or chaw. You best let me do your talkin' about hirin' on. My captain is over there donating his month's wages to that faro dealer. Soon as he's bust, we'll have a talk with him."

"Captain?" Ned asked.

"Well, he was my captain in the Tenth Cavalry. We fought Indians from Arizona to Canada. But now he's the straw boss for the Sleepy Z. We got cattle spread from here to Reno an' it's time to put an iron on 'um. He's needin' help."

Ned and Henry sipped their drinks and talked for almost an hour. Birchtold sat at a table talking in low tones to a couple of others, drinking whiskey and casting brow-furrowed glances at Ned and Henry Clay Hammer.

Finally, a big red-headed man unfolded from a nearby faro table and walked to the bar. "You got enough left for a beer, Henry?" he asked sheepishly.

"Sure 'nuf, Captain. This here's Ned Cody. Ned, this is Captain Preacher Gattlin. Toughest bluebelly and hell-breathing preacher in the U. S. of A."

The red-headed man extended a raw-boned hand to Ned. "Mr. Cody," he said. But he didn't smile until Henry handed him a beer. "Unless you're figgerin' on visitin' Maggy's, and I don't ever remember her extending credit, we might as well head 'em up and move 'em out." Gattlin downed the beer and turned toward the door.

"Captain, Cody here is a hand with stock and is lookin' for an outfit."

The red-headed man stopped and looked at Ned skeptically. "Why would a fine-lookin' young man like yourself be wantin' to eat dust, live on beans, and dig the boils out of a steer's butt?"

"Need the work," Ned said simply.

"You can ride with us t'wixt here an' Bishop. We'll talk more on it there." Gattlin turned toward the door again but Henry called him back.

"Might as well work him along the way, Captain. Say a dollar a day?" Henry appeared to know this Captain well.

"Yeah, yeah, a dollar a day." Gattlin stomped out the door and across the porch.

"He'd a' worked your butt all the way to Bishop for beans and bacon, then hired you on. He didn't get to be captain by givin' the Army's money away nor outfit domo by givin' away the Sleepy Z's. But you're hired on now. I hope you know, gettin' hired and stayin' hired is two different things."

The two Indians still hunkered down near the saloon door, watching the comings and goings and waving away an occasional fly. Ned and Henry swung into the saddle. Gattlin was already mounted and waiting thirty yards down the dirt street. As Ned and Henry reined away from the saloon, a shout stopped them short.

Birchtold had stepped out from beside the saloon, a double-barreled shotgun in the crook of his arm. "Hey, Blackie, you headed back to the hills where you belong?"

The stoic Indians bolted around the corner and out of sight.

Henry unsnapped the flap on his Cavalry holster, but he was at a serious disadvantage.

"See you're taking the pilgrim with you. Does get cold and lonely out there on the trail. You figgerin' on using that young'un to warm your bedroll?" As he spoke, Birchtold slowly raised the shotgun, hoping Henry would go for the holstered Colt.

At first Ned didn't catch the man's meaning. Then it dawned on him. The slur was the worst a man could make. Ned's adrenaline pumped, and he locked his jaw but said nothing. He figured it was Henry Clay Hammer's play.

Ned's old Springfield was in its scabbard, with the butt to the rear of his saddle and the barrel pointed forward. He knew he couldn't pull the rifle in time to help Henry.

He reined the mare around to face the snarling Birchtold, reached down behind his leg to where the breech of the Springfield extended out from the leather wrap, and cocked the carbine. The sound of the hammer startled Birchtold and he looked quickly from Henry Clay Hammer to Ned. Swinging the muzzle back towards Henry he cocked both hammers. "You best ride on out, you uppity nigger. See if you can make some high yellers with that boy."

Ned could see the anger in Henry's eyes, the scarred one bulging menacingly. He sensed that Henry was going to draw, shotgun or no shotgun.

Ned pulled the trigger on the Springfield.

The lead slug passed through the leather scabbard and exploded dirt at Birchtold's feet.

In the second Birchtold turned his attention away, Henry Clay Hammer had his Colt Dragoon in his hand.

Birchtold never got the shotgun leveled. Henry's slug took the tall man in the middle of his chest, flinging him backwards. Both barrels of the shotgun went off and fifty little lead balls whistled their death song, cutting the air between Ned and Henry.

Birchtold, flat on his back in the dirt, kicked once, pawed at the revolver in its holster, blew bubbles in his own blood, and then lay still.

Henry spurred his horse up beside Ned's. "Obliged, Ned Cody. Looks like I owe you a new wrap for that rifle. 'Pears you got a hole in that one."

Ned nodded, still staring at the fallen man. He'd never seen a man killed before, much less been a part of it.

Up ahead, the captain rode across the dirt street to where the local Sheriff had run from his office onto the boardwalk. "Dead man here, Sheriff," Gattlin announced. "Better call the digger."

"What happened?" the Sheriff demanded.

"Fair fight, Sheriff. I'll vouch for my man."

The Sheriff walked over to the body. "Birchtold never could seem to get the slack out of his tongue." He dug through the man's pockets, then looked up disgustedly. "Six bits. It'll cost a dollar to bury him."

Henry Clay Hammer dug into his pocket, pulled his last silver dollar out, and flipped it to the Sheriff. The man pocketed the coin, turned, and started to walk away.

Gattlin called after him. "Birchtold had six bits Sheriff. Don't Henry have some change coming?"

The Sheriff gave the red-headed foreman of Long Valley's biggest ranch a hard look. "I figured it would go to the church fund, Captain. You fellas got a long ride ahead. You better get down the trail before dark."

"I could hang long enough to say a few words over him. Say fifty cents worth?"

The Sheriff didn't look back as he walked toward the undertaker's. "Town folk won't look kindly on a colored doin' shootin', fair fight or no. You boys better ride."

As they cantered out of town, Henry Clay Hammer reined up beside Ned. "You can bean up and bed down at my fire anytime, Ned Cody."

Cody rode beside the black Indian fighter for over a year. He learned more in that year than he had in his previous sixteen. And he made a friend he missed sorely when he left to go back over the mountain.

Ned holstered the big .44, gathered up the reins of the roan, and started on toward Hiram and Augusta Nelson's. He had been early for the Sunday dinner Hiram had invited him to, and had decided to get in a little target practice. Hiram's thirty acres of pasture and orchard were five miles south of town, and the country between them was open with a creek bank offering a natural backdrop.

As the big roan clomped along, Ned's thoughts were only occasionally interrupted by passing farmers, their wagons loaded with goods for the stores in Bakersfield or for the railroad. The horse plodded at a comfortable, lulling walk in the late morning heat while Ned's mind wandered.

He'd loved his father, but felt he'd never really known him. When Ned had returned from Long Valley and Nevada, he'd found his father in the graveyard next to his mother. As had been the case for most of his young life, it was Mr. McGillicutty who'd stood with quiet reassurance, his arm around Ned's shoulder.

But he wasn't the only one who had helped Ned. Hiram Nelson had been more like an uncle than a mere friend of his father's. As soon as Ned reached twenty, Hiram got him a job with Wells Fargo as a freight handler, then later as a station master. But Ned missed the town and its activity. The lonely stage station was no place for him, so at twenty-three he quit the company and moved back home. By now he could handle cattle, horses, and rustle grub with the best of them. He worked at McGillicutty's and lived in the loft for a couple of years, until Hiram needed a deputy.

Fate and a busted hip had cost Hiram his job and gotten Ned his chance. At twenty-five he was considered by most to be too green to be the Marshal of a town the size of Bakersfield. But he'd been at it almost two years and so far he liked the work. He thought he did a good job of it too. Still, he'd never dealt with any real problems — only petty thefts and drunks, and one horse thief in two years.

As he turned the roan into Hiram's barn-yard, Ned resolved that he would have a talk with Hiram about this Tenkiller after dinner.

Mary Beth carefully rolled pieces of chicken in the mixture of flour, sage, salt, and pepper her Aunt Augusta prepared. She enjoyed the ritual of Sunday dinner with her Aunt and Uncle.

Her father and Uncle Hiram sat out on the front porch and rocked and worked their pipes, keeping their talk to the most mundane of subjects. If Frances, Mary Beth's new stepmother, was within a hundred yards of them she would no doubt be eavesdropping.

All of them were still dressed in their church clothes, but none wore them with the stiffness of Mary Beth's stepmother. Frances Nelson sat in the living room near the front door, knitting and trying her best to overhear the conversation the men were carrying on.

Occasionally Frances would walk to the kitchen door and check on the progress of the dinner.

Frances was as stone quiet about her business — and she considered both Nels and Mary Beth her exclusive business — as she was nosy about everyone else's. Mary Beth knew that Frances considered any help offered by Gus as interference. But Mary Beth loved and respected her aunt and uncle, and always listened to their advice.

Mary Beth stood looking out the kitchen window between the chintz curtains, watching a tall straight-backed man on a roan horse pull into the barnyard. She turned to her aunt. "You didn't mention that the Marshal was joining us, Aunt Gus. I wondered why you had Uncle Hiram kill two chickens. You're not up to your old matchmaking again, are you?"

"Of course not, child. But it is time you found yourself a man." Her aunt winked at her. Since the death of Mary Beth's mother, Aunt Gus had done her best to take her under her wing. But Mary Beth was headstrong and independent, maybe too independent. She was her father's own daughter.

Now Mary Beth sputtered with frustration and embarrassment. "If you must ask a young man to dinner, Aunt Gus, why don't you try that new young doctor? Or Sam Spears, the new cashier at the Farmer's Bank?"

"Fiddlesticks," was all she got out of Aunt Gus. She pressed on.

"Haven't you had your fill of men with

60

badges, Aunt Gus? I've watched you worry and fret. Never a peaceful moment when Uncle Hiram was away chasing some robber or horse thief. I want a man who has an office or store job and comes home. Not one who's mingling with those women down on 'L' Street. Or gone." She planted both hands on her hips and shook her head.

"Now look what you've done," her aunt said, laughing, wiping flour off both sides of Mary Beth's flared gingham dress. "Why girl, if I were you, I'd at least look for a man with some spunk. I haven't had the pleasure of greeting the new doctor yet, but if you think that squinty-eyed Sam Spears is any kind of catch . . . then you and I'd better have a talk about men. Oh pshaw!" She ran to turn the chicken, which was starting to smoke in the frying pan.

Frances Nelson was not really a fat woman, but she was broad of shoulder and hip and the flared, petticoated dress she wore fully filled the doorway to the kitchen. Her knitting was clasped tightly in both hands. "I see that young Marshal Cody had turned into the yard. Is this a coincidence, or did you just not bother to mention he was joining us for dinner?

Gus ignored her, but turned to Mary Beth and patted her on the cheek. Augusta smiled a tight smile and winked at her niece. "Child, you're just getting to be more and more like Frances every day."

Frances spun on her heels and walked back to her seat by the door as Gus called, with mild sarcasm, after her. "Frances, you keep an ear tilted toward the porch and when you hear a lull in the men's conversation, call them to the table."

Mary Beth sidled up to her aunt and spoke in a low tone, "Aunt Gus, you just never let up on either one of us. You know that father is very appreciative of the way Frances had taken over the house. And she's becoming a great help in the business."

"Horse feathers! He never let your mother have the slightest say in the business. If Frances McCalester Nelson wasn't the daughter of the president of the second largest bank in San Francisco, your father would not have given her a second —" She bit her lip as Frances stuck her head back into the kitchen.

"The gentlemen are coming to the table."

Ned was as surprised to see Mary Beth as she had been to see him. They exchanged pleasantries but little more as Gus tried to draw them both out with constant chatter. Frances sat stone-faced, making sure she heard every word Nels and Hiram uttered. Only occasionally did she look up from her plate to give Gus or Mary Beth a reproachful glance when they laughed a little too loudly.

The only time Frances spoke was to inform them all, with eyes directed at Ned Cody, that she was going to see that Mary Beth accompanied her to San Francisco to meet some "gentlemen befitting her station," and to introduce her new stepdaughter to San Francisco's opera and the "best families."

After the meal, Ned asked Hiram to accompany him to the barn with the excuse that his horse seemed to be favoring a leg. He was sure Nels would not bother to come along, and he was right.

"Need to chew your ear a little, Hiram," Ned said, as he swung open the heavy, creaking barn door. "We got some trouble on its way to town."

"How's that, Ned?" Hiram crinkled his brow, his full head of graying hair in disarray. He passed a hand through his unruly mop in a vain attempt to smooth it down, focusing his steel-gray eyes on Ned.

"Got a wire from Potter in Wyoming. Fellow by the name of John Tenkiller is supposed to be on his way here. Hiram, you know I'd fight a bear with a switch, if I thought I was right but then again . . ."

"Any man that's not afraid of another man with a gun has got no business wearing that badge," Hiram interrupted, " 'cause he's got no brains! Let's walk a little." They walked out the back of the barn and into the fruit orchard that Hiram was so proud of.

Hiram stopped to relight his pipe. He took two big draws, then pointed the stem at Ned. "I told you when I recommended you for my job, there'd be a chance you might never have to fire that hog leg. But if you ever did have to, then make damn sure you were ready to use it." He puffed on the pipe again and looked at the younger man through furrowed salt and pepper brows. "You been practicing any?"

"Once in a while." Ned cut his eyes away. He knew he had not gotten in near enough time with the tobacco cans.

"Well, you need to spend some time every week burning up some powder. City pays for it!" He winked at his protégé, then continued. "If you know this Tenkiller is comin', I'd go to keepin' that old scattergun close by. It served your father and me well. I seen him blow two fellows clean out of the saddle with one shot one time up above

Linn's Valley. But you hear'd that story a hundred times." Hiram settled into the crotch of a peach tree and spoke in a serious tone. "The one thing you got to keep in mind is this job ain't no game. You're paid to keep the law and that don't mean havin' no straight-shooting contest in the middle of the city streets." He smiled, his gray eyes crinkling at the edges. "Guess I told you about Tom Newberry up in Visalia?"

"No, sir. I don't believe I've heard that one." Ned crouched down and picked up a twig to chew on. Some of Hiram's stories took a little telling.

"Well, a few years back, Tom — he was Marshal then and a real nervous sort. Anyway, he came up against Mean Matt Muldoon in the middle of the main street. Both of 'em totin' six-shooters. Like any careful man, Tom only had five in the spinner. Mean Matt kicked the lid off and turned his wolf loose. They drew down on each other and started emptyin' those hog legs from about seventy-five feet apart." Hiram used his pipe stem like a barrel of one of the revolvers, then smiled again. "One shot creased the barber's bald head, 'bout a block down the street, and knocked him out cold. On the way down he cut off a piece of the feller's ear he was shavin'.

Another of those slugs hit Estes Williams in a place that kept him for sittin' at the Town Meetin' for a couple of months." He slapped his thighs and guffawed. "All that was a bit of a problem for Tom Newberry 'cause old Estes was Town Mayor, and the feller that lost a chunk of ear was on the Town Council.

"Tom empties his hog leg but Muldoon still had one left. Just as Muldoon fired, Tom turned to hightail it out of there and Muldoon's shot creased the back of his shirt and cut his suspenders." Hiram beat his thighs, barely able to get the rest of the story out.

"Well, neither one of those fellers drew a drop of the other's blood till Tom ran Muldoon down and whacked him on the noggin' with his empty gun. I guess he was quite a sight, chasin' Muldoon. One hand holdin' up his trousers, carryin' that hog leg by the barrel with the other, and cussin' hisself 'cause he didn't touch Mean Matt Muldoon with five shots, an' thankin' the Lord 'cause Muldoon couldn't hit him with six.

"Tom got his man, but that didn't keep old Estes from gettin' him fired, while Estes was presidin' at the next Town Meetin' . . . standin' up, a' course." Hiram calmed down and drew on the pipe again. "Last thing I hear'd of Tom, he was punching cows up in Montana somewheres."

Hiram's mood had turned serious again. "You use every advantage you can get. There will always be some cowhand who can shoot the gnats off his horse's ears at a hundred paces, not like old Not-so-Mean Matt Muldoon, and is more than willing to prove it in the middle of Chester Avenue." Hiram struggled to his feet and began to swing his crippled leg back toward the house. "Gus said somethin' about the last of this year's peaches makin' a cobbler."

Just before they got to the front porch, Hiram turned back to Ned and shoved the pipe stem into his chest the last time. "You remind me, I got something to give you afore you head back to town. Might keep you from havin' 'Here Lies Mr. Gnat' cut on a stone over your skinny bones."

Mary Beth worked the pump at the kitchen sink and watched her Uncle and Ned walk back to the house. Ned did cut a handsome figure, she had to admit. Hiram was a big man, even stooped as he was now, and Ned stood a half a head taller. Ned was slender, but not skinny, and he moved like a mountain cat with nary a misstep. His full head of chestnut-brown hair was a little too long and he was always a little disheveled, but a wife could solve that. He had disarmingly soft brown eyes, and a way of looking at you like he knew what you were thinking.

She laughed at herself when she thought of Sam at the bank. He was tall and thin too, but his Adam's apple bobbed when he talked, his long arms and legs stuck too far out of his suits, and he was always stumbling over himself. His slick hair, parted in the middle, only added to his already comical looks. And he had the most disconcerting snort when he laughed, which he did far too often and far too nervously.

She could barely get a word out of Ned. If anything he was too solemn. He laughed and had a flashing grin, but on too few occasions.

While Aunt Gus was dishing up the cobbler, Mary Beth made up her mind she'd try to get a little conversation, and maybe even a smile, out of Mr. Cody over dessert.

CHAPTER FIVE

George Howard stood by his office window and watched his deputy, Puttyworth, crossing Railroad Avenue with a short, chubby Mexican in tow. He'd sent three deputies into the Tenderloin in the middle of the morning to find out what they could about Mr. Tenkiller.

The Sheriff took a seat in his swivel-back chair and propped his feet up on the desk. The door swung open and the chubby man stumbled into the office ahead of Puttyworth. The Mexican spotted Howard and quickly threw back his shoulders, stood up straight, and smoothed his clothes with his hands. Then he ran one hand, spread-fingered, through his long black hair.

"This here's Ricardo Urrea," Puttyworth said, grinning at his boss, one missing front tooth causing a little hiss when he talked. "He's been a guest at the Yuma prison. Seems he took to another man's horse down

Phoenix way a few years back."

The Mexican nervously switched his weight from one foot to the other. His narrow, pig-like eyes took in every detail of the room.

Howard lit up a cigar and let the man squirm for a moment. Though not yet noon, it was already hot outside. But it wasn't hot enough for this man to be sweating the way he was.

"I have paid my time, *señor.* I have done nothing."

"I'll decide what you've done." The Sheriff rose to his full height and blew smoke into the man's face. Howard turned and walked to the window and spoke without facing the chubby Mexican. "Let's see, 'Ricardo' — that means 'Richard' in the King's English —"

"As you say, *señor.*"

"Don't interrupt me, *cholo*!" Howard turned his stare toward the sweating man, whose own eyes noticeable narrowed and hardened.

"Now as I was saying, 'Ricardo' means 'Richard' in the King's English. And 'Richard' is 'Dick'. And your last name's Urrea, that's some kind of piss. So I'll just call you 'Dick Piss'." Deputy Puttyworth guffawed.

70

"So tell me, Mr. Dick Piss," Howard continued, "what do you know about another *cholo* . . . a feller called Tenkiller?"

Ricardo resented being referred to as a *cholo* more than he resented the twisting of his name. Men had come to early California from Mexico, recruited from the prisons of Mexico, mostly Mazatlan. They had been offered a choice: guard the missions of California or stay in jail. These men were the dredges of Mexico, and were known as *cholos*.

But Ricardo was now worried about other things. He shifted his weight from side to side and moved his eyes about the room as if looking for a way out.

"I asked you a question!" The sheriff raised his voice.

"Nothing, *señor*. I have heard of no Tenkiller. It is not a Spanish name."

"Now, boy, if you don't want to cool your heels in my hot little jail, I suggest you remember. I would hate to have this county spend money to wire all the counties 'tween here and Yuma just to see if any of those Sheriffs want you. That could take a month or so, while you're eatin' those good jail *frijoles*."

"No, *señor*. I tell the truth. I have never heard of John . . . of Tenkiller."

71

The big, pot-bellied Sheriff moved as close as he could to the chubby Mexican and bent down almost nose to nose with him. "I never tol' you his first name, *cholo*. How come you knowed his name was John?"

The man tried to pull back, but Putty-worth stood right behind him. He stuttered, "I did not know him . . . but he was there when I was there . . . in Yuma, I mean. But I did not know —"

"You know what he looks like?" Howard shouted into his face, his spittle spraying the little man.

"*Si, señor.* I saw him on work details."

"Well, he's comin' this way. And it seems to me that the likes of him might wander down your way into the Tenderloin. You will keep a sharp eye out for him, Mr. Piss? I'd hate to have to spend the money to send all those wires!"

"*Si, señor.* If I see him, I will tell you, *pronto.*"

"Faster than *pronto,* Mr. Piss."

"*Si, señor.*"

"Get him outta here," Howard snarled.

Puttyworth dragged the little man out through the outer office and shoved him into the hall. When he came back into the Sheriff's office, the Sheriff was standing at his window, watching the chubby Mexican hurry across the street.

Howard spoke without turning back to his deputy. "Good work, Puttyworth." He gnawed on his cigar. "I wouldn't be a bit surprised if Mr. Tenkiller is comin' to town to visit an old friend. Not a bit surprised. You go on and see what else you can turn up."

George Howard sat and pondered long after Puttyworth had left to resume his search. Tenkiller could be very important to him. The election was coming up and he needed some good stories in the newspaper. He needed to catch this man and get him locked up, not merely returned to Wyoming. A good, sensational trial and the opportunity to show up the new City Marshal for the young, flap-jawed, flannel mouth he was could cinch the coming election.

Ricardo Urrea hurried back to Cordova's Cantina, where he'd worked since first arriving in Bakersfield. He dealt faro from a tell box — a box with an intricate mechanism which allowed him to "tell" what the next card would be — and stole from the drunks.

The last person in the world he wanted to see was Johnny Tenkiller. Even as silent and brooding as Tenkiller was, it was hard not to get to know a man when you slept six men to a six-by-eight cell. Now he wished he hadn't told Tenkiller about his sisters in Bakersfield, hadn't spoken of their beauty and success as bar and crib girls, or of his wish to join them as soon as he was released from Yuma.

Ricardo had talked to the man a lot, trying to be friendly. He for damn sure hadn't wanted him as an enemy. Urrea shook off a cold shiver as he remembered telling the pock-faced Apache of the good time they would have if he ever got out of Yuma and came to Bakersfield. Surely the man did not remember. That had been over three years ago.

Ricardo arrived almost two hours early for work, and Hector Cordova looked at him curiously. The *cantina* did not open until eleven, but Ricardo usually started dusting tables and chairs by ten, while sipping a tall glass of *aguardiente*. By eleven-thirty he'd dusted most of the chairs in the place.

Cordova's was on the outside edge of the Tenderloin, beyond the Chinese section and the last building on the way out of town, except for McGillicutty's Livery. As Ricardo got ready to deal the first hand of cards, he

74

wished he were a lot farther out of town. In fact Hermosillo or Mexico City would be just about right.

Alvarado Cuen studied the smoky saloon and wondered why he preferred Callahan's to other places in the Tenderloin. There were only a couple of other *Mexicanos* in the place, and English was the language of preference. The place had filled up as the shadows in the street lengthened. Now that it was full dark, the saloon was packed.

Most of the eating was over and Nelly Mc-Dougle, the pretty little part-time cook and bar girl, had taken her place serving drinks. "I wouldn't do such a thing, Mr. Collins," Al overhead Nelly say. She bumped into him as she hurried by. She seemed flustered and upset.

Bart Collins leaned against the opposite end of the bar from where Al stood. Collins was a surly, sullen man whose tolerance for the bottle was as short as his temper. He was on his fifth or sixth drink, bellied up to Callahan's bar, when he decided that Nelly had short-changed him.

Puttyworth, with Winston close behind, wasted no time coming to Nelly's aid. Puttyworth had been spending a lot of time at Callahan's trying to get Nelly to expand her duties by accompanying him upstairs. This looked like the perfect opportunity to put her in his debt.

He flashed a missing-toothed grin at her and then stepped up behind Collins.

Collins was a medium-height man, but was almost as thick as he was wide — and it wasn't due to fat. He only came to town once a month for supplies, got drunk, slept in the livery, then went back to his mine somewhere up on the Kern. Inside or out, Collins kept a floppy-brimmed hat pulled low over his eyes, covering his thinning carrot-orange hair.

"Why don't you just pay up and find another place to do your drinking, mister." Puttyworth hooked both thumbs in the belt that strapped his big Colt to his waist.

Collins took a draw on his beer, reached under the bar for one of the towels that hung every six feet, and wiped the foam from his red mustache. Then he turned slowly around to face them. Both deputies stood six inches taller than Collins, but neither looked bigger than the broad man. "I been drinkin' here the first of every month for two years, an' I believe it suits me fine. Ain't you two county law? Why don't you wander up to Keene where you belong?" Collins turned back to the bar.

Al watched the scene with interest but stayed where he was. Puttyworth had always been a little on the slow side, and Winston looked to him for inspiration, so it was a moment before either of them reacted.

"I said get on down the road," Puttyworth spat. But it was Nelly who hurried away. She'd worked the bars long enough to know that a woman's presence only caused trouble.

Collins didn't budge other than to lift the little shot glass of whiskey which accompanied his beer and upend it.

All the men at the long bar backed away, except for Collins and Al Cuen. Cuen didn't even lift his head up from his drink, but his eyes watched carefully in the mirror behind the bar.

When the quiet became too obvious, Jimmy "One Eye" Callahan stuck his head out of the kitchen. Puttyworth just stood looking around, not knowing quite what to do. Finally the pressure of everyone watching forced him into action. With Collins still facing the bar, Puttyworth pulled out his heavy Colt.

Collins caught a glimpse of Puttyworth's move in the mirrors behind the bar and spun just as Puttyworth brought the Colt down across his head. The glancing blow knocked his floppy-brimmed hat flying, exposing his bald pate with its carrot wrapper, but the blow barely fazed him. He shook his head once and then, with a blow like a sledgehammer, knocked the much taller deputy across a table. Men scattered, and poker chips, cards, and glasses flew as Puttyworth and the table crashed to the floor.

With a back-handed right, Collins swept the overturned table aside and reached for Puttyworth with his left hand. Wrapping a well-calloused, ham-sized hand around the deputy's throat, he drove two short blows to his face with the other. But the second was unnecessary. Puttyworth was out cold from the first punch.

Winston jumped back out of harm's way, pulling his Colt just as the city deputy, Ratzlaff, came in through the back door. Callahan grabbed for "one-eyed Betsy."

Winston's Colt was leveled at the unarmed Collins, and the ominous ratcheting of its hammer rang through the quiet saloon. There was no doubt about his intent.

Hissing like a viper, a long well-tallowed bullwhip snaked out from down the bar. Winston's gun hand flew up. The gun fired into the ceiling as it leaped from Winston's grip.

Ned sat comfortably with one foot on the floor and the other propped up on his bed in the Southern Hotel. The new three-story facility didn't take permanent guests, but made an exception for the City Marshal.

Ned admired the gun Hiram had given him as he wiped it with a lightly oiled cloth. The Colt Police .36 barely resembled the revolver which had left the Colt factory, as Hiram had cut down both the barrel and grip and removed the loading lever. Now it was only five inches of stubby killing power and could be hidden in a belt or a boot.

Sunday evening had been quiet. A little too quiet for a night with a full moon rising. Ratzlaff had the duty and Ned was glad of it. It had given him the chance to visit with Hiram and get some of Gus's excellent cooking down. He admitted to himself he'd enjoyed Mary Beth's company. Good company and good food and a night off.

He was beginning to doze when the sharp report of a shot snapped him back. Leaping into his pants and boots and grabbing the big .44, Ned headed for the door. He remembered the .36, returned, and stuffed it under his shirt at the back as he bolted down the hall, taking the stairs three at a time.

Al Cuen, recoiling the whip, spoke quietly. "No need for shootin'."

Ratzlaff stepped up behind the tall Mexican. Knowing only that Cuen had disarmed a lawman with his whip, Ratzlaff brought his own heavy Colt across Cuen's head. The big Mexican folded in a heap.

Ratzlaff gathered up Winston's gun, but didn't return it. He neither liked nor respected the county deputies, but he was not about to make his feelings known to a bar full of drunks. He might need the deputy's help sometime.

"Give me my gun," Winston insisted, extending a shaking hand.

"Let's get things settled down here," Ratzlaff said. Ignoring him, he walked to where Puttyworth was now sitting spread-legged on the bar floor. The deputy, blood flowing from his open mouth, was cussing and fingering the spot where he was now missing a second front tooth. Callahan leaned quietly against the back bar with Betsy cradled in the crook of his arm.

Collins returned to his drink as if nothing had happened.

Al Cuen had not moved. He, and the whip, lay still.

Ned Cody burst through the front swinging doors. He quickly surveyed the saloon, noting his deputy Ratzlaff, standing with his .44 drawn but hanging with its business end casually pointing at the peanut-shell littered floor. Ned directed his gaze to Ratzlaff. "What the hell's goin' on here?"

"I think we got it handled!" Ratzlaff extended a hand to help Puttyworth to his feet.

The Sheriff's deputy pointed a shaking finger at Bart Collins's back as the big man stood at his spot at the bar, casually sipping his beer. "He's goin' to jail!" Puttyworth hissed through the gap that was now two teeth wide.

Winston yelled, rubbing the angry red welt on his wrist and pointing to the prostrate Al Cuen. "So's that Mexican! Both of 'em. Give me my gun, Ratzlaff."

Ned spoke quietly. "This is the city, boys. Ratzlaff and I will walk these fellows down to our place. We got room." He crossed to where Al Cuen was beginning to stir, and gathered up the whip.

Ratzlaff spoke quietly to Collins, who still leaned on the bar, a thin red line of blood seeping out from under the brim of his recovered hat. The thick man shrugged his shoulders, walked over, and helped Ned get

Cuen to his feet.

Ratzlaff set Winston's gun on the end of the bar as they headed out the front door, glancing back several times to where Putty-worth and Winston glared after them, before the four of them rounded the corner.

From the alley across from Callahan's, a sallow pock-faced man with a scar on his upper throat stood in the moon shadow and watched the foursome leave the saloon.

"You got no call to be lockin' me up, Marshal," Collins complained, his eyes brown and flat. Al Cuen's, on the other hand, were black and flashing, bulging with anger.

"Best for everyone, Bart. I'll cut you loose first thing in the morning. You won't have to sleep in the hay tonight." The thick man smiled a sheepish grin, walked into the small cell, and flopped onto the bunk, with his hat still in place.

Ratzlaff grabbed Al Cuen by the upper arm and directed him to the second cell. The man didn't budge.

"Move it, *cholo*!"

"My name is Don Alvarado Cuen . . . and if you push me again I will show you how the *vaquero* throws the bulls by the tail."

Ned Cody could not help but laugh, but

Al Cuen never smiled. Ned wondered if Cuen really could throw the huge Ratzlaff. He'd seen Al and his friends at the Mexican rodeo compete with each other for money by upending thousand-pound bulls. The *colear* was a technique that required skill and perfect timing. The *vaquero* rode up behind a running bull, leaned down, and grabbed the tail at its base, then slid the hand back near the end and tucked it securely under his own near leg. A quick spin of the horse at the exact moment and the bull's rear hooves were in the air and the bull was flat in the dirt.

Cuen's comment did not impress big Theodore Ratzlaff, who reached again for him. Ned stepped between them. "Take a seat in that cell, Al. I'll see if I can rustle up some coffee."

The two adversaries stood and stared without blinking. "Get the pot goin', Theo," Cody said. Ratzlaff turned away and Cuen walked quietly into the cell.

"There was no reason for him to club me, *señor,*" he mumbled, sitting on the bunk.

"It all got out of hand, Al. You'll be out with the sun, just rest easy."

"No reason." Al sailed his flat-brimmed hat into a corner.

CHAPTER SIX

The small wooden house had been added to many times in order to reach the still-modest size which housed Gum San Choy's six children, mother and father, and his wife's ancient grandmother. In addition to the cramped living quarters, an area had been set aside for the laundry.

A large brick stove, its middle featuring a built-in wok, separated the laundry from the kitchen and egg preparation area. Gum San had been much too practical to waste the heat from the wood he used to boil the water for the laundry; thus the boiling of eggs was begun. His customers, only half kiddingly, accused him of boiling the eggs in the old laundry water. But he didn't. He'd stopped doing that long ago.

Gum San was an acquired name. Working the fields near the Yangtze River, young Choy would watch the junks sail past on its muddy water and talk of the exotic places he would see when he escaped Jiangsu Province. Escaping was not an easy feat, and talking about it might get you thrashed with bamboo for a first offense, or hung if your talk persisted. The warlord of Jiangsu, Taiping, was not a tolerant man.

Still, many times, young Choy would watch the sun set behind the beautiful Zijin Mountains, named for their purple and gold splendor, and wish for other places and adventures.

When word came that many were leaving for California to seek their fortunes on streets paved with gold, young Choy could not stand it. He talked so much of the *gum san* — "gold mountain," as California was called — that his work mates began calling him Gold Mountain Choy, Gum San Choy.

Finally, risking great shame and ridicule for his family, he left in the dead of night. The great capital of Jiangsu, Nanjing, and the junk he hoped would take him down the Yangtze's broad murky waters to Shanghai, was a two-day walk. He'd taken only a handful of rice. More would have been a burden on those who remained.

He was able to talk his way onto one of the huge rowable, flat river junks, by convincing the captain that he would work for a little rice and fish soup. The skills learned quickly on the river ship came in handy when he reached Shanghai and its great harbor after another two weeks. He talked his way onboard another harbor cruiser that often passed near one of the great China Clippers anchored well out in the harbor.

Gum San dived from the scow's deck and swam for the anchor rope of the big clipper. With a mixture of joy and trepidation, he hand-over-handed up the rope until he reached her broad fore deck. He was greeted by two white-devil sailors who immediately clasped him in irons and hauled him below.

Shaking, wet, and cold, he waited for the rest of that day and a night, until light flooded into the dank hold where he was chained. Two men passed through the hatch.

"Do ye speak English?" barked the taller of the two. Gum San did not answer, for he did not. The other man began a sharp questioning in a dialect that Gum San could barely understand. Soon they reached some middle ground and Gum San was able to explain that he only wished to go to the "great gold mountain."

As they hauled him to the deck, he explained that he would work for his keep as he had no money. He had some glimmer of hope as the smaller of the two told him that a man could earn passage, but only by producing twenty paying passengers. Laughing, they yelled, "Good luck," and flung him over the rail into the cold bay twenty feet below.

Luckily, Gum San was a strong swimmer, and Shanghai was a busy harbor. Another scow picked him up and got him close enough to shore so he could swim to the stony bank.

Deciding that he must be as enterprising as persistent — there was no returning to his family, after all — he set out to convince twenty of his countrymen. After two weeks, just before the *Eastern Zephyr* was to sail, he stood impatiently at the dock with twenty yellow pilgrims, who were, like himself, convinced that riches were merely a matter of walking along and picking golden nuggets from the California fields.

Two and a half months later, with little ceremony, Gum San Choy was deposited into one of the roughest Tenderloins in the world — the Barbary Coast of San Francisco. Even at their worst, the docks of San Francisco were better than the cramped hold where he and 250 of his countrymen had lived in their own filth. Only a near-revolt had gotten the captain to allow them a daily airing and walk on the deck in groups of no more than 25 at a time. The docks of San Francisco were heaven, compared to the dank, dark hold of the *Eastern Zephyr.*

San Francisco was not so much a surprise as was the realization that the "Gold Mountain" was another week's walk away.

After two years of back-breaking work, watching the white devils get rich off the sweat of the little yellow men, Gum San decided there must be a better way.

He started a laundry with a large kettle, a flat iron, and a flat rock to iron upon. By the end of the next year, he was able to send the fare for his parents and for a wife of their choosing. He also sent substantial reparation to be paid to the agent of Taiping, the warlord, for his parents' right to leave. A year after his parents and wife arrived, he sent for her parents and grandmother.

The family followed the gold camps and the railroad camps south. It took the railroad three years to push over the Tehachapi Mountains east of Bakersfield, and the Choy family became well-settled. His wife's parents died. And Gum San decided the family had moved enough.

His wife died during her last childbirth and his mother was too old and feeble to be of much help. His father was full of advice but was able to do little, only to clean the barnyard trash and stains from the eggs before cooking. Old Grandmother sat, and rocked, and smiled.

This left most of the laundry chores to Ling Su, his eldest daughter. At thirteen, Ling Su was as accomplished at the laundry as she was at cooking and directing the egg-pickling process. She was his pride, and his heart swelled as he watched her take on her dead mother's chores.

Gum San stretched and struggled to his feet from his sleeping mat, careful not to disturb his two-year-old son, who managed to sneak onto his father's mat almost every night. Before Gum San had slipped into his sandals, Ling Su sat up, stretching and yawning in the predawn darkness.

By the time he'd stoked up the laundry fire, Ling Su had scurried to his side with a pan of dry breakfast rice and a bowl of prunes. While she cooked, Gum San carried buckets to the pump in the back yard and filled them for the laundry kettles, continually popping sugar candies into his mouth. It was a habit he'd cultivated almost as soon as he came down the gangplank of the *Eastern Zephyr,* one that had cost him all his teeth, earning him the current nickname — Toothless.

He heard a stirring in the long hen house beyond the clotheslines. He stopped pumping the water for a moment and listened. When the cackling of the hens stopped, he continued with his chores.

Gum San finished refilling the kettles just as Ling Su finished her cooking. They ate in silence. She rinsed the bowls and whispered to her father that she was going to gather eggs for the morning's boiling.

The clotheslines were covered with sheets and shirts that hung lifeless in the predawn stillness. Ling Su made her way through the sheets, being careful not to touch them with the candle she carried inside the large flat basket she used to gather eggs.

Two hens bolted, cackling and flapping, from a hole cut in the base of the hen house door. Ling Su jumped in fright. She hated the dark, and even more so the creatures in the dark that might be attracted to the chickens. "An old tomcat," she thought. "Maybe another skunk or coon?"

Ling Su opened the squeaking door.

She held the candle out at arm's length and swept it from side to side.

A dark man stepped from the shadows, clasping his hand over her mouth before she could scream. He slapped the candle away with his other hand, but not before

Ling Su saw the blood that splattered his chin and upper chest.

She bit down on the hand that covered her mouth. The dark man grunted and slapped her hard. She screamed as he pulled her to the ground. He hit her again, harder this time, and with his fist. Ling Su tasted blood in her mouth.

Through the misty haze enveloping her brain, Ling Su realized that the dark man was tearing off her quilted trousers. She felt his weight on her, then smelled his rancid breath in her face.

His hand grasped her breast as his rough stubbled face scraped her cheek and neck. She was terrified but could neither scream nor rise. Beating at his back, Ling Su pulled at her assailant's long, stringy hair with her free hand. She gritted her teeth and made a straining animal sound, squeezing with all her might as he forced her legs apart. She cried out as he entered her mercilessly. The dark man slapped her into silence, growling and pumping for a few moments more. Then Ling Su felt his full weight relax on top of her. Then he lay still.

Rising, he hitched up his breeches. When Ling Su started to sit up, he kicked her heavily in the ribs. As she rolled onto her face Ling Su could smell the slime that coated the floor. Then, mercifully, she passed out.

The man picked up the two dead hens that had sprayed him with blood when he jerked their heads off, and carried them out through the door. Silently he disappeared into the brush.

Gum San thought he heard something above the noise of the crackling and popping fire and walked to the rear door. He stood listening for a moment, then turned and walked back to his work at the kettles.

When Ling Su did not return, he began to worry. It was not like his daughter to dawdle. As he turned toward the door, it opened. Relieved, Gum San turned back to the egg kettle, sputtering as it boiled over.

"Ling Su, we must hurry with the eggs, lazy girl," he chastised, but not seriously. She whimpered and Gum San turned to look at her. Ling Su was leaning on the door jamb, her face smeared with blood. Chicken manure, straw, and filth covered the white padded top she wore. She held her torn and filthy trousers modestly in front of her. Blood dripped from the corner of her mouth, tears streaking the dirt on her face.

His daughter collapsed to the floor before Gum San could reach her. Gasping, swearing at the gods, he knelt beside her. His oath gave way to a prayer when he noticed the blood that streaked her smooth thighs.

CHAPTER SEVEN

Ned's long strides took him briskly down the boardwalk towards his office. He tipped his broad-brimmed hat to the barber and the owner of the dry-goods store as they opened the cast-iron shutters that enclosed the windows of their establishments.

Except for the Tenderloin, the town was locked up "tight as a turtle" at night and only began to show its personality as the tall black-and-green sheet-iron shutters were swung open. Between the Southern, where Ned hung his hat and guns, and his office many establishments were only now coming awake.

The sun had been up for over two hours. Toothless Gum San and his daughter had been squatting outside Ned's door for most of that time.

Ling Su kept her head hung low. Toothless flicked the flame off the end of the crumpled cigarette he was smoking, stuffed the butt carefully in his pocket, then reached out and lifted his daughter's chin. An ugly welt crossed her left cheek. Her left eye was swollen almost shut and was already turning black.

Ned's soft brown eyes hardened. He quickly unlocked the padlock to his office door, stepped back, and motioned his visitors inside. Over the bellowing of Bart Collins, still locked up in the back, the story of the beating was quickly related.

Ned interrupted Toothless and walked to the door leading to the cells. He stuck his head through and yelled. "You fellows will be out of there in a minute if you shut up that belly-achin' and let me finish what I'm about."

"Well, I got a load of supplies to —" Ned slammed the door before Bart could finish.

"Now go on, Gum San."

"Two vely best hens gone, Marsh' Ned. Vely best!" Gum San stammered, shifting his weight from foot to foot. Ned knew that they were probably his worst hens . . . but also he sensed that his little yellow friend was not telling all.

"What else troubles you, Toothless? The hens don't concern me near as much as the condition of Ling Su. That's a pretty vicious beating for a fellow to give over a couple of

Rhode Island Reds. Particularly to a little girl."

"The thief, he . . . he beat Ling Su," the old man stammered.

Once again Bart Collins started bellowing and Ned stomped back to the door. "Dang it, Collins. I'll keep you right there cooling your heels till Christmas if you don't let me be for a minute."

Ned turned, surprised to see Gum San pushing Ling Su through the front door. The Marshal feared the worst, but he knew Gum San had to tell him everything, in detail, if Ned was to do his job. "Wait old friend, I need Ling Su to describe —" But Gum San had already shoved her through the door and closed it behind her. He turned back to Ned.

Gum San hung his head, unable to look at his friend as he spoke. "He has taken her honor," the Chinaman mumbled into his chest.

"He what? Speak up, Toothless!"

"She not be fit wife to any man."

Ned took Gum San by the arm and sat him down on a long bench beneath the window that faced the street. Ned sat beside him. Putting his hand on the little yellow man's shoulder, Ned spoke firmly. "You must tell me everything if I am to help. Tell

96

me what you mean, Toothless."

This time the old man looked him right in the eye and spoke up. "He has taken her as a husband would, and beat her . . . too much."

Ned's jaw tightened. He gritted his teeth in anger, knotting his fists. Rape was a crime far more rare than murder, and was considered even more heinous by many. "Where did this happen, Gum San?"

"In the chicken house. Before the sun."

"Does she know who he was?"

"No, Marsh' Ned. Only ugly man. A white, or brown man. With blood on his face."

"How old is Ling Su?"

"She has thirteen new years. She was born in the Year of the Rat."

"I want you to take her to see Doc Gilroy. He will look at that cut and make sure she is not badly hurt where . . . where . . . anywhere else."

Gum San rose and shook his head. "No, Marsh' Ned. She see Huoy Lee and he treat her."

Ned had seen Huoy Lee perform some wondrous cures with the concoctions of his Auspicious Health Herb Store and did not argue.

"Will you do that now, old friend? I wish

to come to your place as soon as Deputy Ratzlaff gets here."

"Huoy Lee's is on our way home." The old man padded and shuffled to the door. "We be home vely soon. Eggs still not boiled and sheets not ironed. Vely soon."

Gum San pulled the door quietly shut behind him just as Bart Collins let out a bellow that would shame the lop-eared mule he rode. Ned grabbed the key ring from its peg and went to Collins's cell.

"Blast you, Ned Cody," Collins roared. "I got twenty miles a'ridin' and two feet of solid rock to cut through afore my conscience will let me bean up and bed down!"

Ned turned the big key in the cell lock. "You're just damn lucky Theo Ratzlaff came along or you'd be in George Howard's jail. That glory hole o' yours would be full of rats and rattlers before he cut you loose. Not to mention that blacksnake of Alvarado's. You'd likely be toes up, if it wasn't for him."

Al Cuen sat, legs stretched out on the bunk, with his *sombrero* pulled so low over his face you could not tell whether he was sleeping or awake. At the mention of his name, Al pushed the *sombrero* back, wincing as it touched the lump on his head.

"You ready to get down the road, Al?"

Ned asked, opening Cuen's cell.

"I'm ready to step out in the alley with your dog-dumb deputy, Cody." Cuen adjusted the *sombrero,* avoiding the lump.

"I suggest you stay away from Theo. He was only doing his job as he saw it."

"Yes, just as the gringo law has always seen their job. You have my whip?" Alvarado's black eyes flashed.

"I'll get it. You stay away from Theo and Winston and Puttyworth. Winston's totin' a big grudge for you." Ned turned to Collins, who was leaving by the dividing door. "And you beat it on out of town too, Collins. It'll take Puttyworth a couple of days to get the swellin' down. But he'll be roarin' mad when he does."

Collins removed the floppy-brimmed hat and held it in both hands in front of him. "I don't like to be obliged to any man, but I guess I owe you a thank you, Cuen."

"It was my pleasure, *señor.*" Ned recovered the whip from his desk drawer and handed it to Cuen, who strapped it to the back of his belt. Cuen's eyes narrowed. "You tell Ratzlaff, and Winston, that I will be doing my drinkin' at Cordova's, where friends will watch my back. I will be pleased if they would join me . . . any time."

"I got other things to do, Cuen. Right now

I got a low-life, chicken stealin' ra—" Ned decided, for Ling Su's sake, to keep the rape to himself. "I got a chicken thief to catch."

Just then big Theodore Ratzlaff, whose first chore in the morning was to open the town meeting hall, filled the doorway.

"Send him," Cuen spat. "Rats can smell out things the rest of us would miss."

Ratzlaff's eyes narrowed, but Al slammed the door behind him as he left. "What's that all about?" Theo asked.

"Nothing. Get the coffee goin'. I haven't even had a chance to stoke the fire up. I gotta go down to Gum San Choy's place. Somebody stol' a couple of chickens and beat up an' raped his little girl."

"I hear'd those Chinese girls was creased on the bias."

Ned interrupted him coldly. "I don't think you're funny. That little girl is only thirteen."

"I don't know why you get involved in those people's business. You know they'd rather take care of their own affairs." Theodore Ratzlaff placed the Chinese just a little below the Mexicans on his scale of who deserved the attention of the law.

Ned Cody kept his anger to himself. "You mind the shop, Theo. By the way, Al Cuen doesn't have you on the top of his Christmas list right now. He's no back shooter, but I wouldn't give him a reason to pop your ears off with that blacksnake of his. You're ugly enough already." Ned spun on his heels and walked out the door to the stable. It was a mile and a half to Gum San's, and he would need the roan if he was going to do any tracking.

And he planned to track this son of a bitch to hell and back, if necessary.

CHAPTER EIGHT

Ned tied the roan to a plum tree in front of Gum San's house.

One of the younger children ran to take the reins of the big horse and lead him away so he wouldn't eat the foliage. All of the trees in Gum San's yard had a productive purpose.

Ned walked to the chicken house with Toothless. Ling Su had calmed down enough to give Ned a better description of the thief, and now Ned worried that the man might be much more than a robber or a rapist.

Finding the chicken heads where they had been discarded, Ned searched for a sign that the man had hit his own head or caught his hand or arm on a loose nail. Locating nothing more, Ned concluded that the blood Ling Sue saw on the man's face and chest must have been from the birds.

One thing the slimy shed floor did offer

was well-defined footprints. Ned bent down and carefully studied the pad marks of Ling Su's soft shoes and the tracks of a man's boots.

"Look at this, Toothless." He pointed to a left boot-heel print, and then to another, four feet away. Gum San studied them carefully, then shrugged his shoulders.

"He has a cut, a nick, on the outside edge of the heel, like he stepped on something sharp. Won't be another heel like that. At least not with the cut in just the same place." Ned followed the tracks and occasional drops of blood outside and into the brush until he found where the man had mounted and rode away.

As he walked back to the roan, Ned placed a hand on Gum San's shoulder. "You talk this up during your rounds today, especially with the Chinese. Spread the word what this fellow looks like. But caution them, old friend. This may be the man I spoke to you about."

Gum San listened intently and nodded. Ned mounted and rode out to follow the horse sign leading off through the brush.

Johnny Tenkiller cut a river willow, stripped the bark from it, and skewered a hen as soon as he got back to his camp near the river.

While it roasted, he grabbed up a handful of river sand and scrubbed the chicken blood from his chin and neck and, as best he could, from the front of his doeskin shirt. Then he plucked and cleaned the second chicken. He had not eaten, other than a few pan biscuits, since the peach pie two days ago.

He'd spent the night in the alleys of the Tenderloin, looking through windows for his old cellmate, Ricardo Urrea, but he'd had no luck. Tonight he would take the risk of going inside the saloons and walking the streets. He was sure no one in this town would know him, or of him, other than Ricardo.

He gnawed the meat from the bones of the first hen while the second roasted. Suddenly, something triggered a primeval instinct deep inside him and he rolled up the half-cooked chicken inside his blanket, saddled, and rode away. He'd heard no sound nor seen a thing. He'd simply sensed trouble. The quintessential sixth sense of the hunter — and the hunted.

After a mile of tracking, losing the sign twice and having to backtrack and dismount, Ned dropped down onto the river's edge. The water had been receding over the past two months and the sign was clear in the now-muddy courses of the once-high water. He spurred the roan on for another mile. Rounding a thick clump of river willow he spotted a campfire, barely smoldering, only fifty feet away.

Ned slipped quickly out of the saddle and palmed his .44. He slapped the roan on the rump. It kicked up its heels and looked back at him as it trotted on through the middle of the camp. Stepping back into the brush, Ned stood quiet for a few minutes, then began picking his way softly in a circle around the site.

Satisfied that it was abandoned, he crossed to the fire and studied the sign. Chicken bones and grease spots covered the sandy area around the fire, and a muddy spot revealed a print of the cut boot heel.

Thirty paces beyond the camp the roan was grazing on new grass under the overhanging branches of a huge cottonwood. Ned caught up with him and remounted. As he did, he saw a lone rider on a low rise a half mile in the distance. The man sat on a buckskin horse, stone still, watching Ned.

Ned shook off an involuntary chill. Before he could spur the roan, the rider disappeared over the brow of the rise.

By the time Ned galloped to the granite

ledge where he had seen the rider, neither the man nor the tracks of his horse were found. A mile beyond, the edge of town began.

Riding down several of the Bakersfield streets and all of the Tenderloin streets, Ned kept his eyes open for a buckskin horse or a swarthy man with bloodstains on his shirt. Two horses could have been the one he'd seen from the distance but he recognized them both. They were both owned by men who would not be stealing chickens nor raping Chinese children.

Disgusted, he slumped his tall frame in the saddle. Ned Cody returned to his office.

Johnny had ridden right through Bakersfield. He knew from long experience that the best place to hide a tree was in the forest, and a man among a thousand others.

He'd not checked the saloons of Sumner. He'd heard talk of them as he walked the alleys of the Tenderloin of Bakersfield, so he rode out the east side of town and continued on to the railroad depot and the small settlement that surrounded it.

He would look for Ricardo there. And when it got dark, he would return to Bakersfield.

Theodore Ratzlaff was leaning back in Ned's new swivel chair with his hat pulled over his eyes when he was startled awake by the purposeful slam of the front door.

"Theodore," Ned told his bleary-eyed deputy, "see if you can find Denny Saunders. I need some tracings of a poster that Howard got from Wyoming on that Tenkiller fellow." Ned unbuckled the big .44 and hung it on the coat tree.

Ratzlaff grumbled under his breath, but stood and shook out his trouser legs. "Where do you suggest I do that?"

"I'd start at his father's store. You know Saunders? Owns Saunders Mercantile?" Cody said sarcastically. Ratzlaff knew exactly where to find Denny Saunders. The young man was a promising artist and the tracing would be no challenge to him. "Tell him to beat it back here with maybe ten or so. I'll give him a nickel each, if he does a good job."

Ling Su usually delivered and picked up the laundry, but Huoy Lee insisted she lay down for the rest of the day. Gum San had two earthenware crocks of pickled eggs slung from each shoulder, a basket of fresh eggs hanging from the crook of his arm, and a stick across his upper back with baskets of laundry suspended from each end. Despite his wide load, Gum San did not have to turn sideways to walk through the gate of Charley Bok Yue's boarding and joss house.

The joss house was a study in contrasts. The gate was seven feet wide and eight feet tall with a large carved wooden Chinese dog on each side. At the top of the entranceway was an intricate carved crosspiece with Chinese characters spelling out "Gate of Heavenly Pleasure." It opened onto a small yard cluttered with barrels and boxes.

Mounted next to the front door was a large crucifix with a two-foot Jesus — the white man's joss. Its paint fading, the wooden Christ surveyed the boarding-house's comings and goings, demonstrating to the white devils the sanctity of Charley Good Book.

The house itself had many contrasting uses. Floors one and two had fourteen rooms each. Twenty-five very plain pine-walled rooms were rented to boarders — white, brown, and yellow — while one larger room served as kitchen and dining room. Another room was the bath, with a claw-footed leather-lined tub and cast iron stove for heating water, with the luxury of its own pump. Its clatter could be heard the length of the hall but the convenience offset the irritation — at least to those who valued an occasional bath. The necessary facilities were out in the rear yard in a twin-stalled board shack.

On the second floor, the extra-large room fronting the street was the opulent domain of Charles Bok Yue. Charley, known to the whites as "Charley Good Book," had his walls covered in the finest silks, his room filled with intricately carved hardwood furniture, with rugs of embossed Tianjin silk covering the floor.

In the basement rested a huge Buddha. He sat in a room almost as opulently furnished as Charley's living quarters. Buddha, four feet high and almost as wide, surveyed the room with a skepticism equal to the crucified Jesus that hung near the front door.

The middle basement room was a storeroom with furniture and crates and spider webs, all of which Charley was either too frugal or too lazy to remove.

Nearest the front street and farthest from the stairway was a basement room lined with cots, presently occupied with men who were happily indulging in the heavenly pleasures of opium. Smoke lay in a sickly sweet pallor over the cots. The men lolled in blissful retreat, the pupils of their eyes widely dilated.

The joss and boardinghouse was much longer than it was wide. Both its street front and rear were lined with wide porches that were roofed with false verandas at the second level. Railings extended above the porch roofs, but there was no access other than windows. The wide rear porch was a congregating place for the white occupants of the boardinghouse. Only occasionally would a white man venture down the narrow stairs into the basement to partake of the heavenly pleasures. None made the descent to seek Buddha's wisdom.

Gum San had three reasons for calling on Charley Bok Yue. The first and most important was to ask him to watch out for the thief who had stolen his chickens and Ling Su's innocence. The second was to deliver the single fresh egg that Charley insisted on having each morning. The third was to pay his twice-weekly visit to the room across the central hall from Charley's on the second story.

Ge Lu was not a particularly young nor a particularly pretty woman, but she had skills that made an old man happy. She performed them for the laundry and eggs which were required to keep the boardinghouse going. In turn, she paid no rent, with the exception of an occasional visit to Charley Bok Yue's room.

Toothless left his load on the wide front porch and took only a few laundry items, and the egg, to the second floor. He did not like Charley Bok Yue, but he respected him, just as he respected snakes and black widows. Charley was a fat man. His heavy jowls shook as he talked in a Hunan dialect which Toothless barely understood, his fat middle flowing over in the front and sides of the tightly tied waist shawl that bound his silken robe.

Charley was the head of the Chop Lee Tong. Toothless did not approve of the organization's activities and felt they did great harm to the acceptance of the Chinese by the whites. Still, Charley Bok Yue was a powerful man, and not one to antagonize.

Toothless tapped quietly on Charley's door. The big man took his time answering. He surveyed Toothless for a moment, then stepped aside, dropping the Bible he always carried when there was any chance that his visitor might be white. It was a habit Charley had learned as soon as he reached the shores of California — and one which garnered both smiles and trust from the gullible white devils. "You are late this morning, Gum San. Do your hens not honor you with eggs or do you find it difficult to rise in your honorable old age?"

His sarcastic tone was not lost on Toothless. "I have had much trouble, Honorable Yue."

"The white devils do not pay for your services?" the fat man asked. He returned to his wide carved chair and flowed into the seat like cold syrup. Toothless carefully placed the single egg on the small pillow provided for it.

"No, Honorable Yue, even greater troubles." Toothless related the morning's events and appealed to the fat man. "Marsh' Ned has asked that we watch for this man, and come to him if he is seen."

"I do not approve of interfering with the affairs of the white devils. But since she is your daughter, I will take it up with the tong."

Toothless knew he was dismissed. Charley Bok Yue had actually meant that he did not approve of doing anything that he was not paid to do. Backing out the door with a polite bow, Gum San pulled it silently shut. Turning, relieved, he knocked quietly on Ge Lu's door.

She answered. Toothless flashed a gummy grin and disappeared inside.

CHAPTER NINE

The shadows were long in the street by the time Denny Saunders stuck his head in the office. "That dang Cap Colston kept me coolin' my heels in the front office for over an hour," he said crossing to Ned's desk and handing the Marshal a pile of flimsy paper.

"Well, these are worth the wait." Ned counted the flyers and dug into his pocket. "Here's a half dollar for the tracings and an extra dime for the wait. Thanks, boy."

"Thanks, Marshal." The gangling youth scampered for the door, then stopped short. "By the way, whadda' you think about the killins' up near Porterville?"

"What killings?" Ned stopped sorting the tracings and listened intently.

"Well," the boy said, looking a little surprised, "I couldn't help seeing a telegram on the Sheriff's desk. From Sheriff Kelly in Visalia. My father used to . . ."

"Tell me about the telegram, boy!"

"Well, I probably shouldn't have been readin' —"

"Denny, what did it say?"

"Well, some farmer and his wife, just south of Porterville a ways. He was shot out in his barn, and his wife was beat and . . ." The boy looked down at the floor, kicking an imaginary clod of dirt. "And whoever did it took advantage of her. Her clothes were torn off. And whoever did it took a buckskin gelding."

Suddenly Ned was on his feet, leaning across the desk. "Was there any mark on the horse?"

"Didn't say, but it was a big-caliber gun and he was shot three times and she was beat bad. I probably shouldn't have . . ."

"You did right, boy. Sheriff should have told me about this right off. What was the date on the telegram? And who was it addressed to?"

"I didn't notice, Marshal. Shall I go back?"

"No." Ned's serious expression broke into a slight smile as he walked from behind the desk and escorted the boy to the door. "You did right, Denny. Thanks."

As Ned thought about the telegram, heat rose in the back of his neck. After sitting at his desk and drumming his fingers for a few minutes, he went to the dividing door and yelled for Ratzlaff. "Theo, I'm headin' for the printers. You watch the office." He hurried out.

Tenkiller wandered the streets of Sumner, searching its three saloons without success. The trip back to Bakersfield in the black night had been no problem. He tied the buckskin well out in the brush and boldly walked the streets unnoticed.

He pulled his hat down over his eyes and tucked in his chin as he saw badges on two county deputies who were lounging near the front door of one saloon. Johnny turned into the alley alongside the building. Through a window facing the alley he looked inside. A tall lawman, wearing the circled star of a City Marshal, stood occupied at the bar.

Ned Cody was shaking his head from side to side, while Nelly chided him. The sign on Callahan's Chop House had been changed that morning. It now read "Callahan's Chop and Oyster House."

Nelly had waved the Marshal over to the bar, just after he had tacked up the results of his trip to the printers. "You really expect me to eat that thing?" Ned asked the barmaid, who stood laughing behind the bar.

"It's a real delicacy, Ned. Jimmy picks them up, fresh and iced down, every morning at the train station in Sumner. They're real good." She laughed again, covering her mouth with a bar cloth. Nelly enjoyed teasing the tall, handsome Marshal. He was good-natured, and she knew that if she got him started on the oysters, the other men would follow.

Jimmy Callahan walked up and reached for the oyster she'd set in front of Cody. It lay in its shell, shiny, slimy, and patiently waiting. Callahan spooned a little salsa into the shell, and picked it up. "I'm only gonna show you boys one more time." He put the shell to his mouth, sucked the oyster out with a slurp, chewed once, and swallowed. "That's fine. Fine as Sunday mornin'." He patted his belly and walked off smiling.

"It's your turn, Ned. First one is on the house." Nelly deftly shucked another with a long blade knife and laid it beside Cody's beer.

Half the bar was watching as Ned thought, "What the hell." After all, Callahan didn't look any the worse for it. Ned spooned in a little salsa and put the shell to his lips and sucked. He chewed, found little resistance, then swallowed. He chased it with a swallow of beer and looked around at the rest of the bar.

"Why, that's good as Saturday night and Sunday morning." The bar patrons chuckled. Cody turned back to Nelly. "All I could taste was the salsa."

She giggled, moving down the bar to where the rest of the men were crowding up, yelling for the newfangled treat.

Considering his preoccupation with his friend Gum San's troubles and his belief that John Tenkiller lurked nearby, Cody was having as good a time as he could. Tenkiller was more than likely the one who'd called on Ling Su. Cody hadn't voiced his suspicions to anyone, including Theo, but the more he thought on it, the more it seemed to him a fact. The only redeeming thing about the whole situation was that the man had not killed the pretty little girl. He could have. He'd hit her and hit her hard. Tenkiller was getting too close, not only to the town that Ned was sworn to protect, but to those Cody considered friends — almost family. Even though he had never laid eyes on John Tenkiller, finding the murderer was becoming a personal thing. The hair bristled on the back of Ned's neck. For a moment it felt as if the killer was watching him.

■ ■ ■ ■

Johnny Tenkiller took another careful look at the two deputies standing outside Callahan's Chop and Oyster House, then turned to the window for another glance at the laughing law man standing at the bar. Then Tenkiller slipped away down the alley and continued his search for his old cell mate.

He walked back to the street a block beyond Callahan's and strolled along L, admiring the girls who sat in their cribs, winking and smiling at the passing men. There were far more winks and gestures than there were takers. Most business was conducted on Saturday night after the miners and cowhands had been paid. He wondered if one of these ladies might be the sister of Ricardo Urrea.

After he'd walked a couple of blocks, Tenkiller spied Cordova's. It was another block over on M Street, and he crossed a vacant lot between Loy's Shanghai Kitchen and a small blacksmith's lean-to with a Mexican name on the door.

During the four-block walk from Callahan's to Cordova's the white faces were slowly replaced by yellow skins, then mostly brown by the time Tenkiller had reached

Cordova's. Stepping into the dingy saloon, he spotted Ricardo Urrea.

Urrea stood behind the faro table, dealing from his tell box. The three drunks who faced him had no idea that Ricardo knew every card. He let them win the small bets and one out of every three if their bets were consistent. His brother, Enrico Urrea, worked behind the bar pouring beer and *aguardiente* almost as fast as he could move. The place was very busy for a Monday night.

Ricardo was concentrating on his dealing and did not notice the man in the doeskin shirt and dirty breeches who stood behind the players. "What time do you finish?" Tenkiller asked in Spanish.

Ricardo looked up. The sight of Johnny Tenkiller shook him. Stuttering, Urrea answered, "When the players quit." He walked quickly from behind the table and motioned to Tenkiller to follow him to the bar. Then he motioned his brother over. "He's a friend of mine. Take care of him." Ricardo smiled weakly and hurried back to the game.

Enrico sat an *aguardiente* and a beer chaser on the bar, then turned back to his other patrons with neither a comment nor the expectation of payment.

Johnny reached in a crock on the bar and fished out one of Ling Su's pickled eggs. He bit half of it off and, not liking the taste, dropped the unfinished half back into the crock. Tenkiller carefully surveyed the saloon. Satisfied that there was no one there for him to worry about, he wandered around with his beer in his hand. Coming face to face with a tall Mexican, Johnny paused for a moment. Then each took a half step aside and passed. Al Cuen walked outside. He was finished for the night.

Johnny walked to the back door and was surprised to see his own image staring back at him from a poster tacked near the jamb. He instinctively pulled his wide-brimmed hat down over his eyes and tucked his chin. "Damn," he thought, "now I am going to have to stay off the streets."

Denny Saunders's tracing had been printed with a bold WANTED on top and a description underneath. The only addition to the Laramie poster was "suspected of riding a buckskin gelding." But Johnny didn't read well enough to make that part out.

Johnny walked back to the bar and motioned Enrico over. "I'm gonna wait out back," he said. "You keep the beer comin'."

Enrico eyed the unsmiling man and sensed that he did not want to cross him. He nod-

121

ded slightly as Tenkiller ambled out the back door and sat in the dark on the back porch. Now only an occasional drunk on his way to the outhouse would see him.

As soon as Johnny stepped outside, Ricardo hurried over to his brother. "Did you recognize him?"

"Who?"

"Tenkiller! That was Johnny Tenkiller!"

"Jesus, he just walked right in like he owned the place." Enrico shook his head, subconsciously patting the belly gun he wore under his vest.

"Treat him well, brother," Ricardo said. "He is bad. Very bad. We need to talk of this later." Ricardo returned quickly to his game as Cordova, watching the action from the corner, gave him a disapproving look.

It was well after midnight when Cordova decided to throw out the last drunk. It was another thirty minutes before the crew finished cleaning up. Tenkiller waited at the front door as the brothers, the cook, and a pretty bar girl walked out in front of Cordova, who locked up and strode off in the other direction.

Nothing was said for a moment as the three started down the street. Tenkiller broke the silence. "I need a place to roll out my blanket . . . where I will not be seen."

Before Ricardo could answer, Enrico spoke up. "You're a wanted man. It is not good that you —"

Johnny stopped and the other two turned to face him. He spoke quietly, ominously, with one hand resting casually on the butt of the stubby Garland & Sommerville. "You are not a friend?"

The shorter Ricardo stepped between the men and smiled tight-lipped. "Johnny, you know I am a friend. I have not told Enrico of you and what good, good friends we were . . . are. He means nothing." Ricardo looked at his brother and furrowed his brow.

"I need a place to stay." Johnny stared directly into the eyes of the taller man. Enrico held his gaze for a moment, then shrugged his shoulders, turned, and continued walking down the street.

"Of course," Ricardo said. "You can stay with us. At least until we find a better place." Ricardo laid a hand on Johnny's shoulder, then quickly self-consciously removed it.

They continued to Charley Bok Yue's boardinghouse, where Ricardo and Enrico shared an upstairs room next to their two sisters — a fact that pleased Johnny Tenkiller. His pleasure and enthusiasm were not shared by Ricardo. He wanted nothing to encourage Tenkiller's staying. Enrico detested the idea. He did not want the pockmarked man near his sisters, even if they were working girls. He knew the man would not pay, even if he had the money.

For most of that night, Johnny enjoyed one of the main reasons he'd looked Ricardo up. At least, Johnny thought, Ricardo had not exaggerated.

CHAPTER TEN

Ned was in his office early on Tuesday morning. Still he had not gotten there before the first business of the day.

He knew the large, solid man who waited for him outside the padlocked door, but only slightly. Johan Goetting ran one of the last saloons in Keene and came to town occasionally for supplies. The big man extended his hand as Ned approached.

"Marshal."

"Mr. Goetting. What brings you out so early?"

"Not early, Marshal. Even though the saloon business keeps a man late, I've never been able to sleep in. I am mov' my saloon to town. Over on M Street. A block from Cordova's."

"You leavin' the Keene business?"

"Hardly any business left in Keene. Leastways, not enough to suit me and my Siglinda."

Ned smiled. Johann and Siglinda Goetting would be a welcomed addition to any town. They ran an honest place and Siglinda Goetting was one of the finest cooks in the county.

Ned slipped the lock and waved Goetting to a chair. "What can I do for you?"

"Well, Marshal. First off . . . you have no problem with my opening up here?"

"Course not, Johann. Should I have?"

"I run an honest place."

"An' your wife makes the best strudel in the county."

"Maybe da' world." Goetting smiled broadly, then turned serious again. "Now that I am in the city . . . do I still haf' to pay Sheriff Howard?"

Ned sat forward. He spoke carefully. "Pay him for what, Johann?"

"His percentage." The big man's brows furrowed. "I don't t'ink it fair to pay both of you."

"Only thing you have to pay is city tax. An' I don't collect that unless you are way late in payin' it to City Hall."

"Then I still jus' pay the county deputies?" The big man looked relieved.

"You don't pay anyone to be in business in this city, 'cept the taxes I mentioned."

Again the large man furrowed his brows.

126

"Who giv' me protection? What if I haf' trouble in my place?"

Ned rose, walked around to the front of his desk, and sat on the edge. "If you're in my town, it's my job to keep the peace. We make our rounds every day and every night and if that's not enough . . . if you've got some special problem, more often."

"An' no pay? Just a little taxes?"

"No pay, Johann. Just what everyone else pays to keep the peace."

The big man stood, grinning broadly. "You come over soon as we get set up, and Siglinda have a big pan of strudel for you." He turned and headed for the door.

As Goetting pulled the door open, Ned couldn't resist one more question. "Johann, just how much you been payin' George Howard for . . . to . . . to keep the peace?"

"Sometimes twenty-five dollars a week, sometimes more. Not so much lately. Business in Keene is very bad."

"Anybody else there pay Howard to keep the peace?"

"All the saloon keepers and gamblers and the men that keep the girls. If they want to stay in business, that is. Come get your strudel soon, Marshal." The big man waved over his shoulder as he slammed the door behind him.

Ned walked back around the desk and sat down. He grabbed his quill pen and dipped it in the inkwell. He checked the mental calculations he'd already preformed.

If George Howard collected even ten dollars a week from every saloon keeper in Keene during its heyday, each saloon would pay him more than a deputy's salary every month. Then there was Caliente and Tehachapi and Mojave. Ned couldn't begin to guess what the amount might be. But he didn't have to guess about one thing — it was sure as hell against the law.

Ned knew one other thing. He wanted to have a long talk with Hiram before stirring up this hornet's nest.

Cody waited until Theo got to the office, then headed out to the livery to get the roan. The livery was a three-block walk and he was in a hurry, but not so much that he didn't have time to stop and talk with the beautiful girl standing in front of the Jorgenson & Smithers dry-goods store.

As he removed his hat, a lock of chestnut hair fell across his forehead. He brushed it aside. "Good morning, Mary Beth."

"Marshal." She flashed a bright smile from under her parasol. Her arms were filled with packages.

"Ned would suit me better."

"Ned then. Good morning, Ned."

"Can I help you with those packages?"

"That's kind of you, Ned. But my step-mother just went back to get something. I'm waiting for her."

Ned was a little disappointed. He'd hoped she had been waiting for him to catch up with her. If her stepmother was nearby, he knew he'd better act fast.

"Next weekend is the big July 4th shindig. I was thinkin' . . . hopin' you might . . . Well they have the big picnic and I hoped you might —"

"That would be real nice, Ned." She smiled and Cody grinned, glad that she'd helped him along.

"But my stepmother and I are leaving on the afternoon train for San Francisco," Mary Beth continued. "That's why we were buying a few things. Otherwise I would love to. I'll be back in a month or so. Maybe we could do something then. A ride or a pic-nic?"

"Why . . . why sure, Mary Beth. A month or so. Well, you have a good trip." Ned tipped his hat and spun on his heels and started away, aware of the flush in his cheeks. "Damn my dumb self," he thought. "I just spurted it out. If I'd waited, she'd a tol' me that she was goin' and I wouldn't have made such a bumpkin out of myself."

"Ned," Mary Beth called out from behind him. Cody turned. "I'll look forward to that picnic. You promise now!"

"Sure 'nuf." He spun again, hoping she didn't notice the red in his cheeks. But she had called out. And she sounded like she meant it.

Mary Beth watched the tall man stride away and wondered to herself if San Francisco had any men quite as tall or quite as handsome. She was sure it had many who were more sophisticated, but that would come with age. Secretly she wished she wasn't leaving until after the Fourth of July festivities.

Johnny Tenkiller never had it so good.

Carmelita and Esther Urrea had taken him to the claw-footed tub and scrubbed him down, then trimmed his stringy hair. But those were the only complaints they voiced before they allowed him to become the meat in their hot sandwich.

The girls did not relish the thought of the sullen, pockmarked stranger. But their oldest brother, Ricardo, had always taken very good care of them, and if he wanted this man taken care of, they knew how.

It was obvious to them that the man was

dangerous, even before their brothers pulled them aside and told them to be very careful. The fact that he hung his pistol from one bedpost and his big, fearsome Bowie knife from the other gave them a hint as to his character. Even his big Henry rifle lay beside the bed, within arm's reach.

The girls did not begin work until after eight each night, so they had plenty of time to spend with John Tenkiller. But they never spent time without each other's company. They decided they would keep him well-satisfied. As long as they kept the meanness pumped out of him, he shouldn't be too much trouble. They had never known a man who did not respond to that particular female device.

Johnny knew the girls were uncomfortable in his presence and that was the way he wanted it. One girl would not even step down the hall without the other, but Tenkiller didn't mind. They took excellent care of him at Ricardo's instruction.

Tenkiller knew Ricardo well. He had beaten the Mexican into submission in Yuma prison, to the pleasure of the guards who always enjoyed a fight between the inmates no matter how one-sided. Ricardo had become Tenkiller's flunky in jail. He had done what Johnny wanted, when he wanted, and he had taken up the role as soon as Johnny had found him again.

Ricardo's brother Enrico was another matter. Johnny sensed he would be trouble. Still, the man had given Johnny no excuse to do what he sensed would eventually be necessary — to either whip him badly, or kill him. Johnny knew it bothered Enrico for him to lie with the sisters, and he played on it. If Enrico was present, he would pat the girls or take outrageous liberties, purposely rubbing the man's nose in it.

Johnny had been there two days, leaving the room only to go to the claw-footed tub or to the necessary out in the back.

The sun had just risen to near mid-sky. Ricardo lay sprawled out on the bed, fully dressed, while Enrico stood looking out the tall window. They could not help but overhear Johnny's rutting in the adjoining room.

"I do not like this, Ricardo." Enrico spoke quietly, his fists balled at his sides. "This man gets on my nerves. I want him out of here."

Ricardo rolled off the bed and stood by his brother at the window. "As do I, Enrico. But I know him well and I do not want to be the one to tell him he must go. I have not told you the worst of it." Ricardo hesitated for a moment, then continued.

"The Sheriff had me brought to him. A few days ago. He knows Tenkiller is here . . . or at least that he is coming. And he knows I knew him in Yuma."

"And you let him come here!" Enrico raised his voice. Ricardo quickly put a finger to his mouth.

"Shhhh. This man would kill any of us for a *tortilla*. We must be clever. We do not want the Sheriff to know we have him here. Still, I would rather be in his jail than skewered on Tenkiller's big knife." He shivered as an exceptionally loud sound came from the next room.

Enrico snarled and stabbed a finger at his older but smaller brother's chest. "This must stop, Ricardo. We are between the Sheriff and Tenkiller. Like a *frijoli,* we go from pot to fire . . . or whatever the *gringos* say." Enrico shook his head resolutely. "We must turn this to our advantage. Go to the Sheriff. He can take this Tenkiller at night, while we work."

Ricardo began to tremble uncontrollably as Enrico continued, "We might make something for our trouble. The Sheriff is a rich man, and the *gringo* elections are near."

"You go," Ricardo squeaked.

"No, no, it is you who the Sheriff called to his office. There is no need to involve me, or Carmelita or Esther. This Tenkiller is your friend, not ours."

Ricardo pointed to the other room. "He is no man's friend. He will kill me! Skin me like a rabbit!"

"He may kill you anyway. At least this way we stand to make something. If nothing else, we will gain the trust of the Sheriff." Enrico laid a hand on his brother's shoulder, then turned, bent over, and pulled a double-barreled shotgun from under the bed. "If you wish, I will help you solve the problem. You and I can take him. In the bath. He likes the bath."

"*Dios mi,* no, Enrico, put that away." Again Ricardo brought a finger to his mouth, entreating his brother to speak more quietly. "What if he sees? He keeps that ugly pistol with him always. Even in the bath."

"You have killed men before, Ricardo. What is so different about this man? He is flesh and blood."

"Trust me, brother, this man's blood runs cold, like a snake. I will go to the Sheriff."

Just as Enrico slid the shotgun under the bed, the door between the two rooms burst open. Both the brothers jumped like they'd heard the hum of a rattler.

"I want a chicken and a bottle of whiskey. Both of you go." Johnny gave them each a hard look. Both brothers knew it wasn't just a request. Enrico hesitated for a moment, then followed Ricardo out the door.

As soon as they'd left, Johnny yelled to the girls, "Bring your things into this room. And take their things in there." Tenkiller figured he'd been in the other room long enough. The girls looked curiously at each other, but obeyed without questioning.

Ned Cody's conversation with Hiram Nelson was disturbingly unsatisfying. It was Hiram's attitude that what Sheriff Howard was doing was wrong, but that is was out of Ned's jurisdiction and better left alone. It seemed to Ned that the whole Nelson family was out to frustrate him this morning.

He decided that, jurisdiction or no, what Sheriff George was doing was wrong, and he was going to let Howard know it.

Cody stomped down the hall of the courthouse and into the Sheriff's office. Cap Colston looked up from his cluttered desk as Ned stomped by. "Hold on there, Marshal, you can't —"

Ned's cold glare shut the man up instantly. Cody then shoved open the door to the Sheriff's private office and stormed inside.

George Howard looked up from the *Southern Californian* he was reading. "Well, Ned boy. What brings you to the heart of county government?"

"Johann Goetting was in my office this morning," Cody said. "He's gonna open up down on M Street." George Howard reached into his desk drawer for a cigar. Then he got up, walked over, and closed the door.

"That's good. Johann's a good, honest operator." Howard sat back down in his chair and propped his feet up on his desk.

"We both know what *he* is," Ned spat back. "He wanted to know how much I was gonna charge him to 'keep the peace'."

Howard bit off the end of his cigar, lit it, then blew a smoke ring. "Well, how much *are* you going to charge, Ned boy? If'n you ask for too much, then my boys won't get their share. That would make my boys real unhappy. Things have been a little tough anyways."

"Johann and Siglinda will be paying their city and county taxes, just like all the good, honest folks do. And that's all they'll be paying to do business in my city."

George Howard rose and walked over to the window, pausing a moment before he spoke. "When did this get to be 'your city', Ned boy? I been 'round this county all my life. Most of my boys been here long as you.

It's our city too, an' don't you be forgetting. This city is just one city in the county." Big George Howard faced Ned, chomping down on his cigar, and hooked his thumbs in his broad belt. "And it's *my* county," he added with finality.

Ned walked to the door. "Nobody in this city is going to pay anything to anyone that's not approved by the City Council. And nobody in the county should be paying anything to anybody if it's not approved by the Board of Supervisors. You keep your boys in the county and I'll take care of the city."

"You stay in the city, boy. And you stay away — and I mean *far* away — from the Board of Supervisors!" Howard chomped down hard, nearly cutting his cigar in half.

Ned locked his gaze on the bulging eyes of the red-faced fat man, then turned and exited, slamming the door a little harder than necessary.

Cap Colston jumped, turning his head as Cody stomped across the office and into the hall. He quickly turned away as Ned glared at him before slamming the outside office door, also a little too loudly.

As Ned Cody crossed Railroad Avenue, Ricardo Urrea was making his way down the tracks and across the rear yard to the back door of the courthouse. He quickly slipped in and headed down the hall to the Sheriff's office.

Cap Colston looked up but did not stand as Urrea entered. Quickly Urrea removed his hat and held it with both hands.

"*Por favor,* I need to see Sheriff Howard."

"Sit down. I'll check to see if the Sheriff has time to see you." Cap went back to what he was doing and left Ricardo sitting until he finished. Then Colston walked into the Sheriff's office.

"That Mexican is here. The one Puttyworth dragged in the other day. You wanna see him?"

Howard looked up from his desk, then walked to the peg on the wall that held his gun belt. Strapping it on, he nodded his head in the affirmative and waved Cap out.

The Sheriff was sitting at his desk with his feet propped up, when Ricardo entered. The Mexican stood quietly, shifting his weight from one foot to the other as Howard looked up from the wanted posters he appeared to be studying.

"Well, Mr. Piss! What brings you here?"

"Tenkiller. Johnny Tenkiller. You said to come —"

George Howard was instantly on his feet. "He's here?"

138

"Y . . . yes," Ricardo stuttered. "He . . . he's at Charley Bok Yue's. You know, Charley Good Book's? But my sisters and my brother are there. You cannot —"

"Who else?"

"Just the regulars. He came alone. Sheriff, I did not know he was com—"

"That don't matter, Ricardo. You did good. You wait outside." Howard shoved him roughly through the door and yelled at Cap. "Round up the boys. All of them. And do it pronto."

George Howard went back to his desk and grabbed a cigar. He walked to the window and watched Cap scurrying across the street. "This might be better than just catching one killer," he thought, scratching the liver spots on his balding head. "Might be a whole lot better."

By the time Cap had returned with Winston and Puttyworth, Howard had it well thought out. Johnny Tenkiller, chubby Dick Piss, and his brother Enrico would be the solution to all his problems.

Cap and the deputies hurried into Howard's office. George Howard smiled. "I don't need you boys just yet."

"Cap said that this Tenkiller was here," Puttyworth sputtered.

"If you fellows see John Tenkiller, you go

139

the other way."

"But —" Winston managed before Howard shut him up.

"No 'buts' about it. You leave him be. I want this done right. Just exactly right. You boys go back to what you were doin'. Remember, leave Tenkiller be." It didn't have to be repeated. Neither Puttyworth nor Winston would call up John Tenkiller without plenty of backup. Then Howard went on, "I'll let you know where and when. Now get back to whatever." Then, as an afterthought, he added, "If you see Tenkiller leaving town, come runnin'. Cap, send Ricardo in."

Ricardo was pleased with the new respect he was receiving from the big Sheriff. This time the Sheriff asked him to take a seat, and closed the door to the outer office.

"Ricardo, you been around town a long time, haven't you?"

"*Si, señor.* Except that one time in Arizona." Urrea flushed a little, then continued. "My family has been here and in Pueblo Los Angeles for many years. Three generations."

"Well, Ricardo, you have no idea how much I appreciate your coming to me with this information. I appreciate it so much that I'm gonna' give you some money. Some *big* money."

Ricardo smiled and leaned forward in his chair. The Sheriff continued.

"I got me a little problem here in the city. It seems the Marshal . . ."

It was more than an hour before a very wary Ricardo Urrea left the Sheriff's office. He glanced nervously from side to side, like an overly fed but still alert ferret, and returned to Charley's boardinghouse.

CHAPTER ELEVEN

Ned was tired, but it was a weariness born of frustration. He'd walked the streets of the Tenderloin for most of the afternoon, keeping an eye out for a pock-faced man and a buckskin horse.

So far two buckskins and a dun horse had proven to belong to a sheep man, a drummer, and a miner — and none of them even slightly resembled John Tenkiller.

A ride out to Gum San's had proven fruitless. Ling Su poured him a hot cup of tea, which was the last thing he wanted, since it was so hot in the July sun that one of her eggs would have baked in his hat.

She remembered nothing more of the man who had attacked her, and it was probably just as well. Gum San had told Ned that Ling Su had been crying out in her sleep every night since the man had been there. To Gum San's chagrin, the other children now had to gather the eggs — after daybreak

142

as they too were afraid of the dark. This gave him a late start and made many of his customers unhappy.

Toothless also reported that none of his inquiries about the man had resulted in anything. The Chinese community was very close-knit, and had they seen anyone who fit the description of John Tenkiller, Toothless would have known about it.

When Ned returned to town, he wished he could just go straight to his room. But he still had work to do.

Ned turned the roan over to a stable boy. Flipping the boy a dime, he ordered, "Give him a full measure of oats and rub him down good."

The boy merely nodded, leading the animal off as Ned made his way to his office. It was his night to make rounds, and he wasn't looking forward to it.

Cody found Theodore Ratzlaff at the basin in the back room that housed the cells, stropping a straight razor and lathering up a mug of soap.

"You goin' to church, Ratzlaff?"

"Hardly. Since it's your night on the firin' line, I'm gonna see if I can catch me a little somethin' to take the pressure off."

A little disappointed, Ned had hoped to trade Theo night rounds. Now he wouldn't even bother to mention it.

Ned sighed. "I'll probably see you out there."

Theo slapped on so much lilac water that Ned could have tracked him by his scent. The deputy pulled on a clean shirt and waved over his shoulder as he passed through the door. Both the big man's shoulders nearly touched the jambs, and he had to duck a little so that his hat would clear.

Cody sauntered to his desk and plopped into the swivel chair. He almost never drank on duty but decided he would need a little something to get him through to midnight. He ran his finger around the inside of the coffee cup that had rested on his desk since Johann Goetting had been there that morning. Wiping out the coffee smudge, Ned reached into the back of the bottom drawer of the desk. The little pumpkin-seed flask was half empty, but the half remaining was enough snakebite medicine to cure what ailed him. Ned emptied the flask into the coffee cup and took a generous slug.

The .36 was chafing his calf. He'd devised a leather strap that held it securely in place with the butt just below his boot line, but it needed adjustment. He'd rework it tomorrow, he decided. It wasn't the only thing in life chafing him. And certainly not the most important.

Other than his .44 and his shotgun, Ned's horse was one of the few things Cody had of his father's — and Ned valued it highly for its sentimental value as well as the fact the roan was an excellent mount. He felt guilty about not taking care of the roan himself when he'd brought him in.

Years before, when his father had died, Mr. McGillicutty had cared for the animal until Ned returned to Bakersfield. One of the many things Ned's father had done well was train horses, and the roan was a good example. The big mount handled almost as well with guidance by the knees as he did by the reins, and that could be a handy thing if a man had to fire a long gun from the saddle. The animal was also broken to the report of gunfire. Ned could remember his father firing blank loads around the animal at all kinds of odd times. Now the roan barely flinched when a weapon was fired, even from on top of his back.

The sun was just down. The town would usually begin to roar as soon as the late sun set on a summer night. It was already after seven.

As he sipped the last of the whiskey, Ned's thoughts wandered to John Tenkiller. He

145

wondered again if the man he'd seen on the buckskin horse had been the half-Apache, half-Mexican killer. Odds were the man was not even coming to Bakersfield. But keeping the peace was Ned's job and he had to keep on searching. Thinking about Tenkiller, Cody crossed the room and took the Parker scattergun down from its pegs. He pulled a cleaning cloth from his desk drawer. The Parker also had been a bequest of his father — one that his father had cared for with almost the same devotion that he'd given the horse.

Cody finished cleaning the Parker shotgun and sipping the whiskey at about the same time. There were times when he'd rather be fishin', and this whole week had been one of them. He propped his feet on his desk and thought about a little stream he'd found in the high mountains above Porterville. It crashed and roiled through the deep fern-blanketed shadows of the Redwoods and was filled with trout. Ned had promised himself he would return there. Just he and the roan. Get the hell out of this heat before the summer was over. Cody dropped his feet from the desk top, rose, stretched, and strapped on his .44. Then he walked out to see what the night would bring.

■ ■ ■ ■

Ratzlaff had already decided that Tuesday
night was about the worst night a man could
pick to go out on the town. Callahan's
saloon was occupied by three cowhands and
a drummer playing poker at a table, two of
the town's unmarried merchants lounging
at one end of the bar, with old Whiskey
Lem, the town's most dedicated drunk, sag-
ging across the other.

Nelly McDougal tried to interest Theo in
oysters, raw, fried, or steamed, but he
steadfastly refused. He hadn't yet tried the
new specialty of the house, and he wasn't
intending to do so.

Theo stood watching the poker game for
a while. He killed three whiskeys, then
decided he smelled way too good to be
wasting it on a bunch of cowhands and a
snake-oil salesman. He left the saloon and
wandered down the street.

Half the street-fronting cribs were closed
down. The other half was filled with girls
doing their knitting, or darning stockings,
or just sitting together talking. They hardly
looked up as Theo passed. He couldn't even
get a rise out of the ladies of the night.

Ratzlaff stuck his head in Sill's and

White's, and decided that it was even deader than Callahan's. Sauntering down the alley to M Street, Theo noticed a lantern on in a building that'd been locked up tight for over a year. He flipped the thong off the hammer of his Colt and stepped quietly inside.

Johann Goetting knelt on his hands and knees hammering tin patches over knotholes in the floor while Siglinda Goetting stretched high washing the insides of windows. "Howdy," Ratzlaff said.

"Alo, Deputy," Johann smiled at Theo. "Grab a hammer and I give you lesson in pounding nails."

"You folks gonna open up here in town?"

"Didn't Marshal Cody say anything to you? I stopped by to see him dis morning. Come in, come in and I buy you a drink. After we open you have to buy your own, but now, here." He poured Theo a water glass full of whiskey, then returned to his work. Ratzlaff watched for a while, then slugged the glassful down and said his good-byes.

Goetting accompanied the deputy to the door. "You come back when we get open and I give you a big piece of Siglinda's good strudel. No free drinks, but a piece of strudel." He laughed as Theo waved.

The three drinks in Callahan's and the big water glass of whiskey had made Ratzlaff a little tipsy. He laughed at himself as he stumbled off the porch and started on to Cordova's.

Ratzlaff paused at the double doors. Ricardo Urrea had two unsuspecting players at his table. His brother, Enrico, stood casually behind the bar reading the paper. Theo snorted as he spotted a tall man standing at the center of the bar with Cordova's pretty little bar girl. Ratzlaff thought the tight embroidered pants and waistcoat of the *vaquero* were a little on the fancy side. Men should wear leather and canvas, and fur if it was cold enough, not pretty "doo-dads."

Alvarado Cuen, his hat pulled low, leaned on the bar and spoke quietly with the bar girl. The far end of the bar was occupied by three loud men. Puttyworth, Winston, and Big Jim Jackson had obviously been there for a while. Jackson was the deputy that George Howard had posted to Mojave. He was as mean as he was big and could handle the railroad men, pimps, whores, and gamblers who worked near the railhead.

Cordova sat at his usual table, sipping a beer, eyeballing the action and wishing business was better.

Normally Ratzlaff would have bellied up to the bar for his drink. But to antagonize Cuen, he took a table and yelled to the bar girl, "How 'bout a little service, *señorita*?"

The girl hurried over to the table and Cuen became aware of Ratzlaff's presence for the first time. Alvarado had already stared Winston down. He remembered Ned Cody's warning but figured it was just as well to face trouble when it comes, since it always catches up with you anyway.

Cuen and Ratzlaff locked eyes for a moment. Then the bar girl stepped between them to take Theo's order.

Discreetly turning back to the bar, Cuen signaled Enrico to bring him another beer. He needed no trouble from the law, and Cordova's was beginning to look like a lawmen's convention.

Ratzlaff quickly downed the double whiskey. Walking to the faro table, he began offering advice to the two *vaqueros* who had been losing steadily. His continued harassment flustered Ricardo, causing him to lose a big hand.

Ricardo said nothing to Theo, even though he'd developed a distinct dislike for the big man. The last thing Urrea needed was someone taking an interest in his tell box.

Again Theo yelled at the girl, "Hey Chile

pepper, you too busy to shag me a drink?"

The girl got another whiskey from Enrico, and quickly took it to Ratzlaff. The hair on Alvarado's neck bristled, but he gained control, deciding that discretion would be wise with the odds as they were. He waved a hand at Cordova, tipped his wide, flat-brimmed hat at the girl as she returned to the bar, and started for the double swinging doors.

Theo Ratzlaff had never been a very good drunk. Ned Cody had cautioned him about his off-duty drinking more than once. The rest of his family had never touched a drop.

Theo's father had been one of the few white men who had arrived in California prior to the gold rush. Fleeing Russia, he had made his way to Sitka, and then on to Fort Ross. Always at odds with the authorities, not legally but politically, Theo's father kept moving deeper into California, eventually settling in the fertile central valley. Many followed him. Eventually a small settlement of Russian Orthodox farmers was established.

As Theo grew up, he watched other white, non-Orthodox families settle in the southern central valley. Theo began to realize how strictly he was being raised and resented it. He left the family settlement and moved

151

into town. Liquor had not been a part of Theo's strict Russian Orthodox upbringing. He had still not learned to handle it. A surly, mean drunk, Theo drank without a trace of humor.

As Al Cuen passed, Ratzlaff could not help but antagonize him. "Hey Mex, is that your lady?"

Cuen stopped and turned slowly to face the seated Ratzlaff. "As far as I know, she is no one's *señora*. But she is a lady, and I am sure that she would prefer we talked of something else."

Theo guffawed in a nasty way, but dropped the subject of the bar girl. "How 'bout that bump I gave you? You want to talk about that?"

"You mean when you sneaked up behind me? Blind-sided me?"

Theo bristled. Rising from the chair, he knocked it clattering across the floor. His gaze locked with Cuen's.

The bar fell silent.

The three county deputies at the end of the bar set their beers down. They started moving down the bar towards the two men.

Ratzlaff held up his hand. "You boys go back to your beers. I can handle this myself." He gave them a hard look, stopping them in their tracks.

"You don't need your friends?" Cuen said, glancing down the bar. He backed towards the door. "Do you need that Colt?" Cuen rested one hand on the whip at his back fully expecting Ratzlaff to draw on him.

"All I need is these two hands, Mex. I'll just get rid of this iron." Theo walked over, pulled the big .44 out of its holster with two fingers, and dropped it with a thump on the bar. "Don't need this either," he added, pulling his deputy's badge out of his pocket and dropping it alongside the .44.

Hector Cordova rose. *"Hijos de putas,"* he mumbled quietly under his breath. He yelled to the squared-off men, *"Amigos,* go on out in the street!"

Enrico dropped his paper and reached under the bar to grab a double-barreled shotgun with one hand and a two-foot bat with the other. At the same time, Al Cuen dropped his whip on the bar, carefully watching Ratzlaff.

Cuen didn't know if Ratzlaff was coming at him or starting for the door, but it didn't matter. He wasn't about to let the big man get in the first lick.

As Ratzlaff stepped forward, Cuen stepped into him. Cuen's overhand right cross took the big man high on the forehead with a resounding thump. Ratzlaff shook it off, but

Cuen quickly followed with a straight left that knocked the surprised deputy back. The right straightened Ratzlaff, splitting his eyebrow, while the left reddened his nose. Both blows had sobered the huge deputy.

Bellowing like a bull, Theo dove into Cuen. They tumbled into the nearest table, sending it crashing to the floor, the chairs spinning away in every direction.

Cuen rolled with the bigger man, ending up on top. He quickly broke away and got back to his feet. Al was not about to get tied up with the massive Ratzlaff.

Knowing that speed was his only chance, Cuen stepped in quickly as Ratzlaff tried to rise. With a sharp right, he snapped Ratzlaff's head back. A left followed, stunning the big man.

Cuen put everything he had into the next right. The blow resounded through the saloon, snapping Theo's head to the side. Everyone knew that big Theodore Ratzlaff would be out cold when he hit the floor.

But the big man rolled deftly, regaining his feet. He grinned at the Mexican, spat out a mouthful of blood, and spoke. "Ain't never been knocked down before! You ain't bad for a little fella." Cuen was as tall as the deputy, but without Ratzlaff's bulk.

Hector Cordova took advantage of the

lull. "*Señors. Por favor,* would you step out
—"

Ratzlaff again charged like a bull. Cuen
tried to duck, but a surprisingly deceptive
blow caught him solidly on the chin. The
Mexican was lifted off the ground as the
deputy buried his ham-like left deep in his
midsection. A smashing overhand right followed, knocking Cuen spread-eagled to the
floor. Gasps echoed from the men in the
bar. The barmaid had scrambled out the
back door with the first blow.

Ratzlaff, convinced it was over, turned
back to the bar to recover his things. But Al
Cuen rolled to his knees and struggled to
his feet, blood flowing freely from his nose.
Ratzlaff shrugged and turned just as Al
lunged into him again. A quick left and right
snapped Ratzlaff's head back. Then Cuen
dove into the deputy's midsection with a
head butt. Ratzlaff doubled, gasping for
wind, and Cuen came up with a hard knee
to the chin.

The blow echoed through the room. Ratzlaff straightened again.

Another devastating right knocked the big
deputy sprawling against the bar.

Cuen stalked him like a cat, circling. With
his back to the three county deputies, he
stepped in again to try to land another blow.

But Ratzlaff covered up, buying time in order to regain his composure.

Cuen stepped back, looking for another opening.

Winston, thinking his fellow lawman was down and out, reached over the bar and grabbed the bat out of Enrico's hand. With Cuen's back to him, Winston swung, holding the bat with both hands. The blow glanced off Cuen's head as the Mexican ducked to charge again. He went down like a bag of rocks.

Ratzlaff shook his head in surprise. Snarling, he took two steps and hit the smiling Winston hard. The county deputy went sprawling over the bar, crashing to the floor at Enrico's feet.

As the Mexican bartender stared at Winston, moaning on the floor, Big Jim Jackson reached across the bar and wrenched the double-barreled shotgun out of Enrico's hand. To Ratzlaff's surprise, Jackson leveled it on him. Theo stared into its ominous twin barrels. "You shouldn't be swinging on the law, boy," Jackson said.

Theodore Ratzlaff's jaw dropped. "But, I *am* the law!"

The third deputy, Puttyworth, chimed in, "You may be the law in the city. But the city ends out in the middle of M Street,

Teddy Rat. You're in the county, boy."

Enrico slopped half of his beer on Winston and the deputy sputtered and came around. He got to his feet, blood gushing from the smashed flesh on his cheekbone, and focused his eyes. Recovering the bat, he climbed over the bar, breaking the locked gazes of Ratzlaff and Big Jim Jackson. "Turn around, you bastard," Winston said to Theodore Ratzlaff.

The huge City Deputy Marshal, still stunned at the turn of events, didn't move. Jackson took a menacing step toward him and motioned at him with the ugly scattergun.

"Turn around, like the man says." Jackson motioned again.

When Ratzlaff did, his lights went out.

Ned Cody quietly pulled the livery door shut. He'd filched an apple from the fruit bowl in the lobby of the Southern and paid a visit to the roan. Just for safe measure he put a couple of handfuls of oats in a nose bag and waited patiently for the horse to mouth the last of them.

By the time Cody walked the streets of the Tenderloin, everything was quiet and most of the places were shut down. That suited him just fine.

CHAPTER TWELVE

"You were not truthful wit' me, Marshal."

Ned Cody was surprised to see Johann Goetting standing at his front door again early Wednesday morning.

"Hold on now, Goetting," Cody said, while trying to get his key into the lock. "Is that a polite way of calling me a liar? Why do you think I was not 'truthful'?"

Cody swung the door open and motioned the German inside.

"You told me I wouldn't ha' to pay the Sheriff. Last night Puttyworth and Winston told me I had to pay, ever' week, just like Keene."

"I told you that all you had to pay was city taxes, and that is all you have to pay." Ned walked over and considered stoking up the little potbellied stove for coffee. But it was already too damn hot for coffee or the fire.

"That's not what those other deputies

said. They said ever' week."

"Those boys are county deputies. They have no business in the city, and as soon as Ratzlaff gets here, I'll mosey on over to the Sheriff's office and get this straight. You're welcome to come along, if you want."

"No, thanks. But I would appreciate it if you would drop by. Let me know what, and who, gets paid." The big man disgustedly opened the door and started out. Then he turned back. "You may ha' quite a wait. I saw those county deputies, with Ratzlaff throwed over the back of a horse. They were headin' for jail wit' your deputy and some Mexican he had tangled wit'."

"What . . . what do you mean headin' for jail?"

"Said they was throwin' both 'em in jail. I only know wha' they tol' me, Marshal."

Goetting slammed the door. Before the echo stopped, Cody was outside with key in hand, relocking the office door.

Ned stomped through Cap Colston's office without being announced. George Howard, Puttyworth, and Winston turned in surprise as the door was flung wide. "You got Theo in your jail?" Ned scanned the three of them.

George Howard leaned back in his chair, his fingers entwined across his broad belly.

159

"That's what my boys tell me, Marshal. Seems he was disturbin' the peace and assaultin' one of my men. In the county . . . not *your* city."

"Is he all right? I hear he came in over the back of a horse?"

"He's fine. Just a little knot on his hard head," Winston offered.

"I want him out. Now."

"He'll get out. In good time." The Sheriff got to his feet as his two deputies guffawed. Cody glared at each in turn, and each promptly regained his previous serious composure.

The Sheriff motioned the deputies out. "You boys go on about your business. I got some serious talking to do with Marshal Cody."

Winston and Puttyworth both touched their hat brims. "Yes, sir," Puttyworth hissed through the space where his front teeth had once been.

When they had left, Howard turned back to Cody. "Take a seat, Ned boy." Cody remained standing. "You want a cigar?" Cody shook his head. Howard ignored his refusal, dug a cigar out of his drawer, and stuffed it into Ned's shirt pocket. "Sure would be better," the Sheriff continued, "if'n we didn't have these problems 'twixt your boys and mine." Howard smiled a tobacco-stained, toothy smile. "Gets down-right embarrassin', your boy bein' in my jail."

"Then let's get him out. Now." Cody took the cigar out of his pocket and tossed it halfway across the room into a wastebasket.

Howard ignored him. "Things is real tight, now that the railroad workers is all spread out. Soon they'll be out of the county al-together, an' we won't be makin' enough to make ends meet. Sure would be better if'n we could work together?"

"Howard, what you do in the county is your business. As long as I don't hear about your botherin' any of the law-abidin' folks that live in the city. Right now, I want my deputy out."

"Cody, a man either rides with the brand, or against it." George Howard looked at him hard.

"Let's go get my deputy out of *your* jail, Howard. Ratzlaff an' I don't ride for any man's brand. We keep the law."

"Well that's too bad, Ned boy." Howard made his way to the door. He yelled to Cap to take Cody back and to tell Ratzlaff that he could roll up.

Ratzlaff and Cuen had awakened in ad-joining cells. They had not said a word to

161

one another. Not that Theo had been quiet by any stretch of the imagination. It was a surprise Ned had not heard his bellowing at his office four blocks away. Ratzlaff had finally shut up when Cap Colston informed him that there would be no breakfast as long as he was carrying on. And next to his freedom, Ratzlaff loved his plate full more than anything. Al Cuen's head hurt so bad he could barely stand the yelling. But it was only slightly less painful than having to open his eyes and speak himself.

The county jail had ten cells in a long row in the basement. Theo was at the cell door the instant he heard footsteps on the stairs. " 'Bout time you got here," he snarled at Ned as Cap turned the large skeleton key in the cell door. Ned ignored him, looking at the man in the next cell with his flat-brimmed hat pulled low over his eyes.

"Al? Alvarado Cuen?" Cody called to him. Carefully and slowly, Cuen lifted the brim. "Cuen, you look like you got a close look at the bottom side of a stampede." The whole left side of Cuen's face would have put a violet to shame. Ned turned back to Theo, who had bumps and cuts on both sides of his face, an eye that was half closed, and a lip that looked like old liver. "An' you look like you stuck your head in a hornet's nest."

Ned turned back to Cap, who had started back for the stairs. "Him too." Ned motioned at Cuen.

Cap hesitated, looking quizzically at Ned. "Sheriff Howard didn't say anything about —"

"I said him too. Now, Colston!" Ned rested his hand on the butt of his .44.

"I s'pose if you say so, Marshal," Colston mumbled, returning to Cuen's cell.

Alvarado rose shakily to his feet. The three men waited in the hall for Cap to bring their things. Ned looked from one to the other. "What happened?"

They both shrugged.

Out in the street, Ned walked between the two men. "What the hell happened?" he asked no one in particular.

"Jus' a friendly little tussle, Ned," Theo replied. "Al here an' me was just workin' off some steam."

"That shouldn't have got you locked up in the county jail. Seems to me it would take a hell of a lot more than that." Cody looked at Al Cuen for an explanation. Still, the tall nut-brown man remained silent.

"Guess they didn't 'preciate me knockin' ol' Winston over the bar. Must a' made 'em spill their beers or somethin'."

Al Cuen stopped in the middle of the

163

street and looked at Theo. "When . . . when did you swing on Winston?" he asked.

"Right after he lollygagged you with that club Enrico keeps 'hind the bar." Theo turned back to Cody. "I tol' that peckerwood Winston that our little discussion was twixt Al an' me. Private-like. That deputy from Keene laid down on me with Enrico's double-barrel and made me turn my back on 'em. That's when he took that bat to me, I guess." Ratzlaff turned to Cuen. "He rapped you so hard, I was kind a' surprised to see you this morning. Thought you might be toes up, pushin' up daisies."

"Well, I'm seein' two of you. And one of you is big enough. I'm gonna find a hole and heal up." Without another word, Al turned and walked off toward Cordova's.

Theo called after him, "I'm gonna be seein' those boys again. When they ain't got that double barrel."

As Ned watched Cuen go, he shook his head. Mumbling more to himself than to Ratzlaff, he said, "He's a strange one."

Ratzlaff smiled. "Don't know 'bout strange, but I can speak for tough. I hit him hard 'nuff to knock out that roan horse of yours and he hit the floor like a block of ice. But he came right back up. He put me down. First time."

Ned looked at the big man curiously. "First time what?"

"First time I ever been knocked down. An' a Mex too." Ratzlaff shook his head.

Ned laughed and thought, Theo'll never change. As soon as they entered the office, Theo made his way to one of the cell bunks. The back room began reverberating with his snoring almost as soon as Theo was horizontal.

Ned pulled his pewter inkwell from a drawer and scraped a little dried ink from the quill with his fingernail. Hesitating, Cody almost decided to return both well and quill to the drawer.

Then carefully, but resolutely, he began composing a note to the clerk of the Board of Supervisors.

It was the first time he'd gone against Hiram's advice, Ned realized. Johann Goetting's appearance and his story of the deputies' insistence that he continue to pay off Sheriff Howard had been Ned's first surprise of the day. That was topped by Ratzlaff ending up in the county jail. Ned knew that Theo would want to even the score with all three deputies, with his fists, if he was given a choice. But more importantly, Ned Cody could not let it pass. It was a breach of lawman etiquette. More than that, it was

165

a political challenge that Cody could not let go unanswered.

But neither of the morning's revelations was as surprising as the petite knock at his office door. Ned was deep in thought, staring at a copy of the John Tenkiller poster. He yelled gruffly, "Come on in, it's open."

A lovely cream-complected, smiling face peeked through the crack in the door. "Ned, I just stopped by to let you know I didn't leave." Mary Beth was as pretty as the picture of John Tenkiller was ugly. Ned scrambled to his feet and went to the door, removing his hat at the same time.

"You're supposed to be in San Francisco. Come in, come in." Ned swung the door wide and motioned to the chair across from his desk.

"I really shouldn't. This is probably not right. My coming here, I mean." She flashed Ned a demure smile and stepped inside.

Ned properly left the door ajar. A single woman would normally not be in a room alone with a man, unless it was her father or a minister. Mary Beth smiled at his boyish chivalry, and took the offered seat.

"What kept you here? I thought you were off to the opera?"

"Well, two things kept me. I've been there a few times with Father and . . . promise you won't tell . . . but I really didn't look forward to a month alone with my step-mother. And" — she smiled mischievously — "a very tall, handsome man asked me on a picnic. Is that offer still open?"

Ned stammered, "Why . . . Why, sure. You bet."

"Wonderful." She rose, her petticoated yellow dress swinging wide as she returned to the door. Ned jumped to his feet to escort her, still somewhat in shock.

"Saturday then?" Mary Beth extended her hand. Ned didn't know if he should shake it or kiss it, so he just held it a moment. She covered the lower half of her face with the fan she carried, and waited for his agree-ment. Her liquid blue eyes paralyzed him. Again she prompted the tongue-tied Mar-shal, "What time are you going to call?"

"Well I . . . what time? Well . . . what time does the picnic start?"

"Are you telling me the City Marshal doesn't know what time a civic function starts?" she teased. Ned flushed. He stepped to his desk and started shuffling through papers.

"It's here somewhere . . ."

"How about noon?"

"Oh. Fine, Mary Beth. Noon is just fine. I'll hire a carriage from the livery."

After leaving his office, Mary Beth scurried back to the dry-goods store where her father was picking up a bundle of cedar shingles. A boy loaded the bundle as her father negotiated his way up onto the front seat of the buckboard. "Well, did the Marshal's office know what time the fireworks start on Saturday?"

"Marshal Cody was in, Papa. He said just after dark."

"I told you. Same every year." Nels whipped up the two matched grays that he used for both buckboard and carriage.

"I never should have doubted you, Papa. You are almost always right." Except about Ned Cody, she thought.

"We got to go by McGillicutty's and pick up some strapping for the busted tack on the carriage. And I gotta get somebody to set these shingles. Summer's the time to fix the roof, not winter. That's closin' the barn door after the horse is out, so to speak." He nodded to himself as they rode down the street. "I'm glad you didn't go, daughter," he blurted out suddenly. It was the first time he'd spoken about her decision to let her stepmother go on to San Francisco alone.

"Me too, Papa. The Fourth of July just wouldn't be the same without you." She smiled and laid her head on her father's

168

shoulder.

Nels beamed.

Johnny Tenkiller was bored. He paced the room and walked repeatedly over to the window.

Stopping, he stared at the young Chinese girl who walked down the alley almost directly beneath the Urreas' second-story window. He smiled knowingly to himself. He was almost sure it was the same girl. Carrying two baskets of heavy laundry, she turned onto the street, then hesitated and spoke to two Chinese who lounged on the front porch.

It was her. He was positive. Now he was glad he hadn't killed her as he probably should have. She could be of use again. Turning, she disappeared in front of the boarding house. Johnny walked to the door of the room and waited for footfalls. He would have some more of that, if she came upstairs into Charley Good Book's.

His wait was fruitless. He went back to pacing, even more frustrated and nervous than before he had seen the girl.

Long minutes passed. Again he stopped at the window. A carriage had reined up in the street by the alley. A well-dressed older man was talking to the two Chinese. In the carriage next to him sat the most beautiful woman Johnny had ever seen. He felt the heat in his loins. Now *she* would be worth risking a run-in with the law, he thought. He watched the carriage drive away, then hurried out and down the back stairs. But by the time he made the street, the carriage was nowhere to be seen. But Johnny would remember her. This town wasn't that big. He would see her again.

He would find out where she lived.

"God damn his scrawny hide. That corks it."

George Howard stomped around his office. Cap Colston had just informed him that Cody had sent a formal note, requesting a place on the agenda of the next County Board of Supervisors meeting. Cap Colston had been courting Amy Richards, the fat, freckled, redheaded County Clerk, and now it had paid off. The ink was barely dry before the note was on Cap's desk, and Cap didn't bother to knock as he brought it to George Howard. Luckily, the note had not stated the reason for Cody's requested time before the Board of Supervisors, and that meant there was still a chance to do something about it. And Sheriff George Howard had already planned for just such a problem.

"Cap, I want to see Charley Good Book, then Ricardo Urrea. Then get me Winston and Puttyworth."

Fifteen minutes later George Howard stood at his window watching Charley waddling across Railroad Avenue, his silk robe dragging in the street and his Bible clutched in both hands in front of him.

Colston closed the office door behind Charley and left the two men alone as he sensed his boss wanted.

"Sit, sit, Charley. Good to see you." Howard went to his desk for a cigar. He offered one to Charley, who took it and shoved it in an inside pocket of the robe. It would bring a nickel from one of his boarders. He shrewdly appraised George Howard, knowing the big man wanted something.

"You look well, honorable Sheriff."

"Not as well as I could, Charley. We got a little trouble here in town. Guess you know about it, though?"

"No, I jus' try an' keep my honorable guests happy. Not to get 'volved in trouble."

"Well you are involved this time, Charley." George Howard let his statement sink in. He had no way of knowing if Charley knew Johnny Tenkiller was stowed up in one of his rooms, but he would bet he did. Not

171

much got by Charley Bok Yue.

It was better if Charley did not know. The fewer that knew the better. That was not the reason he'd brought the man in. He pressed on for the answer he really wanted from the clever Chinaman. "You got tunnels, Charley? Tunnels that lead out of your place?"

"I know of no tunnels, Sheriff." Charley had answered a little too quickly and too positively. Howard knew for sure of at least one tunnel that led from Charley's basement to the ruins of a burnt-out blacksmith shop. The man who had run the abandoned shop had been the only Chinese blacksmith George Howard had ever seen. He had done intricate decorative ironwork as well as mending wagon wheels and shoeing horses, but he'd moved on to growing Pueblo Los Angeles when a fire had wiped him out.

If it hadn't been for the fire, George Howard would never have discovered the tunnel. It was almost a hundred yards long, and changed directions twice, before ending up in Charley Bok Yue's storeroom.

Most of the Chinese had come to California as miners, and digging tunnels in the rich deep soils of the central valley was no chore for them. They believed in a back door, a way out, if the white devils ever turned on them.

George Howard wanted to know if it was the only tunnel out of Charley Good Book's cellar.

"Now, Charley, we have always been friends haven't we? I want you to tell me about your tunnels?"

"No tunnels, Sheriff."

George Howard sighed, sat in his swivel chair, and looked towards the window. "Do you know what aidin' and abettin' a fugitive is, Charley?"

Charley's eyes widened and he clutched the Bible more tightly to his fat stomach. He shook his head slowly.

"Well, Charley," Howard continued, "aidin' and abettin' is about ten years in the state prison, that's what it is. An' you're doin' it." George Howard blew a cloud of smoke in Charley's direction.

Charley excitedly rattled something in Chinese, then stood shaking his head from side to side, causing his pigtail to dance behind him.

"Sit back down, Charley, and don't talk to me in that Chinee. Speak the King's English." Charley promptly sat, but perched on the edge of the chair. "Now, you got a fugitive stayin' in your boarding house. You remember how old Judge Ferguson hung those three Chinee boys for stealin' that burro a few years back?"

Charley blanched whiter than the pages of his Bible.

"Well, he's still sittin' on the bench, an' I don't think he likes you Chinee much." Howard paused again for effect, then walked over and laid a hand on Charley's fat, silken-shoulder.

"Now, Charley, tell me about your tunnels."

Johnny Tenkiller paced the floor.

The food was good and there was plenty of it. He slept well, cushioned between the buxom sisters in a store-bought bed in the fanciest boardinghouse he'd ever been in, which wasn't saying much.

Maybe that was it. He was used to sleeping outside. More than likely, it was being cooped in one place so long. He was beginning to feel caged. And he had been caged too often. He had made up his mind long ago he would never be locked up again.

Johnny unconsciously rubbed the scar on his neck, and remembered the rope that had caused it.

A little band of horses had been grazing down an arroyo towards a spring. They'd followed a belled gelding and were an average-looking bunch, except for a large, young pinto that had not been cut.

The gray mare Johnny rode was favoring a foreleg, and had almost given out. The posse that was chasing Johnny could not be far behind. He'd lost them in a rocky canyon, but if they were any kind of trackers they'd pick up his trail soon.

Johnny was always surprised when the *gringos* got so excited over a little robbery. He had not even killed the man this time — merely pistol-whipped him when he didn't turn over his sack of money quite fast enough.

Waiting behind a mesquite, Johnny easily dropped a loop over the young stallion's neck. Getting a saddle on him was not easy. The young horse had not yet been broken to the bit. As Johnny tried to bridle him, the horse threw back his head, biting at his captor. Johnny got an arm looped around the horse's neck and sank his teeth in the stallion's ear. Then he put all his weight on its head, taking the big horse to its knees. He tied a Spanish hackamore in his lead rope, got it around the pinto's nose, then managed to flip the line behind the horse. The rope led from the pinto's nose, under his tail, and back to his neck. Tenkiller cinched the rope tightly until the young horse's nose and neck were pulled into a half turn. He kicked the horse repeatedly behind the fore-knee each time the pinto tried to rise.

The horse fought the line until he was lathered. Finally, he rolled into the gravel of the arroyo and lay, doubled up and choking and foaming at the mouth.

Johnny found a shady spot and waited.

After an hour, the horse was spent and Johnny easily bridled him. The rest of the little band of horses made their way back to the meadow where they had grazed every afternoon.

Their owner, *Señor* Jesus Gutierrez, was very proud of his stock. He and his sons had captured or traded for what was now a substantial band. They were a major part of his income, and he and his sons worked hard training them. It was Gutierrez's habit to check on them each morning and after-noon. And this afternoon the pinto was missing.

Gutierrez walked from the meadow to the adobe *hacienda* he'd built with his own hands from bricks of mud and straw mixed by his wife. Their first son had been strapped to her back as she stomped mud for the bricks. Now three tall sons and one rapidly growing occupied the sprawling adobe.

Jesus called to his youngest, who was

gathering mesquite for his mama's cooking fire.

"Chico, while I saddle up, you fetch your brothers from the lower pasture. The pinto that I promised you did not return with the band."

"Oh, Papa. I hope the lion who made the great tracks behind my goats did not get him." Chico hurried to climb on the burro he'd ridden for the past two years, and rode to get his brothers.

"*Pronto,* Chico," Jesus called after his son. He knew the boy would be very unhappy if anything happened to the pinto.

Five riders from the small Gutierrez spread galloped out to look for Chico's horse.

The pinto was giving Johnny trouble as the horse regained his strength. He kicked up his heels and sidestepped, and ducked his head and tried to rid himself of the hated load. But Johnny was relentless. He twisted an ear, struck the pinto in the nose with his fist each time he turned, and beat him mercilessly between the ears with the heavy dragoon .44 Tenkiller carried.

Johnny kept the horse at the bottom of a steep ravine, so the pinto's direction would be controlled by the sidewalls. He was so preoccupied with the horse, Tenkiller failed to see or anticipate the ambush.

A *reata* dropped over Johnny, jerking him from the saddle. He tried to pull the .44 but the men were on him instantly. The butt of a Springfield knocked him senseless.

When Johnny awoke, his hands were bound behind him. Four men and a boy sat on their haunches waiting for him to come to.

"Buenos dias," Johnny said casually.

"Not for you, *amigo,*" the oldest of the five men said. "That was Chico's pinto you stole and he is very angry."

"You would not have an *hombre* walk, *amigo*?" Johnny smiled at the men. They all wore large straw *sombreros* and *serapes,* and had the calloused hands of working men.

Again the old man spoke. "No, *amigo.* A man should not walk. But a coyote does not ride. I think we take this coyote to town and see if the Sheriff can teach him about the marks on horses." The old man stood, motioning to the others. They dragged Johnny to his feet.

Johnny purposely stumbled, vying for time. If they took him to town, the *gringos* would have him and he would be back in a cell. He couldn't stand being caged again.

He strained at the leather thong that

178

bound his wrists. Slowly they began to loosen.

One of the men set his Springfield aside to pull Johnny to his feet.

Johnny got a hand free, and drove an elbow to the ribs of one man, then backhanded another, whipping his eyes with the rawhide strands.

Diving for the Springfield, Johnny rolled, and brought the rifle to bear on the old man. But two others were on him instantly and wrenched the weapon from his hands.

The rifle fired as they pulled it away, and one of the men went down. Blood flowed from his side.

Surprised, the second man loosened his grip long enough for Johnny to struggle free and break for a nearby mesquite thicket.

Before Johnny could reach it, the old man rode him down. Tenkiller sprawled in the dust while the other three men pinned him. Again his hands were bound.

"You should have settled for town and the *gringos, amigo.* Now you have drawn the blood of a Gutierrez." The old man dismounted and walked over to his fallen son. The wound would not kill him — not if he was lucky and it didn't fester.

The old man nodded at Johnny and motioned to his sons. "Get him on a horse."

At first, Johnny hoped they were going to take him to town. But they didn't ride.

Instead, the old man looped his *reata* over a greasewood growing from the cliff wall of the arroyo and tied a simple loop in the end.

Johnny began to get the idea. "You cannot do this, *Viejo*. I only rode the horse for a while. I would have turned him loose at the next water hole. I needed water."

"You just left water, *amigo*. How shall I mark your grave?"

Johnny heard the sound of approaching hoofbeats and fought for time. "You cannot do this. I need a priest."

"I think you have not had the need of a priest since you were baptized, *amigo*. If you were baptized. Enough of this. I have honest work to attend to." He started to dismount, then hesitated as the hoofbeats grew near.

The approaching posse rounded a bend in the arroyo. The old man had not yet tied off the end of the *reata*. He still held it in his hand.

"Hold on there, friend." The man who called out led five others, and wore a badge. "Looks like you're doing my work."

"We hang this coyote, Sheriff. I was going to bring him to you so you could dirty your rope, but he shot my son. And he stole Chico's pinto." The boy nodded his head in agreement.

"I got to take him back to town, Jesus," the Sheriff said. "The judge will take care of him. All we wanted him for was a robbery. Now maybe we can get a hanging out of it." The Sheriff started forward.

Johnny spurred the horse, hoping he could pull the *reata* free from the old man's hands. But Jesus was a *vaquero.* He'd taken many dallies around the pommel of his well-worn saddle and did so again.

Johnny was jerked from the horse. He hung kicking for a moment. Quickly the Sheriff drove forward and knocked the old man's hands free of the dallied *reata,* flipping it off the pommel.

Johnny dropped to the ground, choking and coughing, burned deeply where the *reata* bit into his neck.

Tenkiller wound up in the Yuma prison. At times he almost wished he'd chosen the rope.

Johnny rubbed the scar on his neck as he walked to the window of the Urreas' room.

Seeing nothing of interest, he stretched and pulled on his boots. After Ricardo's sisters left for work, after it was good and dark, he would take the chance of going outside. Maybe he would be lucky and see that girl again.

Enrico and Ricardo had been strangely quiet. That bothered Tenkiller some, even though Enrico seemed to be going out of his way to stay out of Johnny's sight and had expressed no more concern about Johnny's relationship with the sisters. Even when Tenkiller pinched one or pulled one down on his lap, Enrico just turned away or went on with his reading.

Johnny wondered where the Urreas kept their money. He'd searched both rooms completely but had found nothing of value other than the old double-barrel shotgun.

But it was handy to know it was there. Johnny was sure the time would come when he could use it.

CHAPTER THIRTEEN

"Now I tol' you before, Ricardo," Howard assured the frightened Mexican. "I'll send the boys off huntin' you up north. You an' Enrico can head the other direction, for Hermosillo, with enough gold in your trousers to last the rest of your days."

George Howard watched Ricardo fingering two fifty-dollar gold pieces. "One for you and one for Enrico," he said. "The rest will be in your saddlebags when you get there."

"I don't know, Sheriff." The Mexican eyed Howard nervously, turning the octagonal coins over and over in his palm.

"I tol' you to call me George. Nine more of those in each saddlebag. Five hundred dollars in gold for each of you."

"This is just too risky, Sher . . . George." Ricardo extended his hand toward Howard, offering the coins back.

"I shouldn't have to tell you this again,

Ricardo. You got no choice. You can hightail it out of town, with my boys latherin' up horses behind you and with no gold . . . Or you can do it my way, and have the posse lookin' for you up north and your pockets full of gold. You ben holin' up that killer for almost a week."

"But you ask me to, *señor.* I came to you an' —"

"That don't cut nothin' with me. You broke the law when you let him in. Now you do it my way and you and your brother will be livin' high on the hog in Hermosillo."

Ricardo shoved the coins in his pocket. "You will have the horses waitin' and the gold in the saddlebags?"

"Eighteen more shiny fifties. They're right there in that ol' green safe. They'll be waitin' for you boys. Just don't miss."

Returning to Charley's, Ricardo took the back stairs two at a time. Enrico had taken the girls to the dry-goods store, but it was getting late and they should be back by now. Soon the girls would have to dress for work.

Ricardo used the signal knock that Johnny insisted on, then pushed the door open. Enrico lay sprawled on the bed, reading the paper. The door to Tenkiller's room was closed.

"We need to talk," he said softly to his

brother. "Outside."

"No problem. He's not here."

"What?" Ricardo almost fainted. He crossed to the adjoining door and flung it open. The girls were dressing but there was no sign of John Tenkiller.

"Where is he?" he shouted.

"Quiet down. The last thing we should worry about is that he has gone. Good riddance." Enrico rose and walked to the window.

"You call ten years 'no problem'?"

Enrico spun to face his brother. "Ten years? What are you talking about?"

Ricardo pulled the door to the sisters' room closed and flipped the gold coins onto the bed. "We must have him here for a while longer. I just came from the Sheriff and he has left us no choice."

Enrico's earlier look of relief, motivated by Tenkiller's disappearance, turned to one of fear as Ricardo related the afternoon's discussion with Sheriff George Howard.

Johnny saddled the buckskin and picked his way upriver. It was getting dark, but a waning moon was rising and he would have no trouble making his way.

He needed money. It was time to leave this place and he would feel better if his pockets jingled.

It had been so much easier when he was a boy in Arizona. He and his father had made or hunted most of what they needed. Money had always meant trouble for him from the first time he'd learned of it. All a man really needed was what Johnny had left behind in the Arizona desert as a boy.

But that was long ago, in another time. Now Johnny's life had again become simple: just take the money to buy what you cannot take.

He reined up as he neared his destination. "Hold up, horse," he commanded. John Tenkiller had never named any animal he'd ever owned. It didn't make sense to put a name to something that you might have to eat someday.

Tenkiller saw the light in the window of the ferryman's shack in the distance and set his mind on the work at hand.

Alvarado Cuen was glad his huge black stallion was still tied and patiently waiting outside Cordova's. The horse had a mind of its own and refused to be taken advantage of. The stallion had busted more than one set of braided reins and many a lead rope when left tied up too long. Cuen looked at the horse with pride, glad that he and other

186

vaqueros rode stallions. Geldings or mares were for women.

The Mexican cowhands were a proud breed. Most of them claimed to have pure Spanish blood, but most were *mestizos.* The blood of Aztecs and Yaquis did not dilute the pride of the Spanish. If anything, it strengthened it, adding even more fire.

But now Alvarado Cuen felt his fire was burning low.

As he slowly mounted, the stallion sensed his rider's condition and did not sidestep or kick up his heels. They plodded along for two miles until they reined up in front of a long, low, adobe *hacienda* on the outskirts of Sumner.

Al could not remember when he had not known Tia Carlita. She always stayed just as he remembered her from when he was boy, with the exception of the gray streaks in her raven-black hair. She had always been fat. So fat that her massive breasts strained at the fabric of her blouse like two bronze watermelons. The flesh on the bottom of her strong arms flapped against his sides as she hugged him, her powerful embrace making his throbbing head feel as if it would burst.

"Ayiii," Cuen moaned. "No more hugs, please, Tia. Just a place to lie down for awhile." The huge woman stepped back and smiled at him. The only thing in the place bigger than Tia was her good nature. And occasionally her temper.

Tia Carlita had known Alvarado Cuen all his life, and had loved his father, Don Lorenzo Cuen, at least on occasion, before Al's life had begun.

"Any place." She smiled at Cuen warmly. "Take any room, *muchacho*. We have no business now, and won't have until later in the day. Have you eaten?" She didn't wait for an answer. "Chapa," she called to one of the girls who stood across the courtyard. "Fetch some *frijoles, carne,* and *huevos* for Don Alvarado Cuen."

"You are my savior again, Tia. And I love you, every big, beautiful pound of you." Al pushed open the nearest door and a girl in a white, lace-trimmed, low-cut blouse arose from where she had been sitting pulling on long net stockings. She placed one foot on the edge of the bed and enticingly completed fastening the stocking with a garter. She flashed a smile at Al, motioning him towards the bed.

Cuen extended a hand palm outward, pleading. "No, no, *gracias, señorita.* Another time. Only rest now." The girl looked hurt, but it was obviously feigned. She winked at

Tia Carlita as the madam waved her outside.

"You will take the food here?" She pushed Cuen onto the narrow four-posted bed and started pulling his boots off.

"If I can eat, Tia. I am very dizzy." Al lay on the bed while Carlita stripped him naked. He was deeply asleep before the food arrived.

The sound of a guitar wafted into the window of his room, and Al Cuen dreamed.

He was back at Rancho Pornicula, "the Ranch of Laughing Waters." His proud, tall, graying father stood on the porch of the big *hacienda* and directed the *vaqueros* to their day's duties.

The fence of the training corral was tall and made of adobe. It was a wonderful place for a young boy to sit, to watch, and to learn.

Ramon Valenzuela was the *segunda*, the foreman, of the fifteen thousand acres of Cuen land, and had been for as long as young Alvarado could remember. He was tall and straight, like Lorenzo Cuen, Al's father, but Ramon's peach-pit face was as weathered and craggy as the granite faces of the nearby cliffs of the Sierras. To the young boy, Ramon seemed as old, as wise, as strong, and as lasting as those mountains.

The horse the *vaquero* worked was a raw-boned, Roman-nosed palomino. The rest of the *vaqueros* had already nicknamed him Caballo Loco, "the crazy horse." And he came by the name honestly. The big stallion kicked and threw his head, refusing the bit as if it were a red-hot branding iron.

Al listened to the comments of the men and wondered why Ramon bothered with this particular horse. The boy yelled from the fence, as the palomino tried again to bite the man who had him tied. "Why do you trouble yourself with this one, Ramon? There are thousands more on the ranch. The *vaqueros* say this one is *loco* and cannot be trained."

The foreman walked to where the boy sat, pushing his *sombrero* back off his head until it rested on his back, hanging from a finely woven strap.

"*Muchacho,* men — and — boys who think a thing cannot be done should not interrupt the man busy doing it. *Momentito.*" He beckoned the boy to wait and walked back to the horse. Giving the palomino enough of the *reata* so he could almost reach the fence of the round corral, Ramon tut-tutted until he had the big horse circling at the end of the woven leather.

"This golden horse does have a little fire of the devil in him. This is not a bad thing, for he has so much more. See how he arches his proud neck? See how high he raises his knees when he trots?

"Remember, this stallion is the son of the horses that came here with Cortez. Horses that fought the fierce Aztecs. The Aztecs thought the horses were gods, until they killed one in battle.

"Remember, *muchacho*" — Ramon furrowed his craggy brows at the boy on the fence — "a proud horse, a horse such as this stallion, will do your bidding. He will carry you places that you would have never seen without him."

He drew the horse up close to the center post of the corral and tied him off, then walked over to the boy.

"He will charge a company of dragoons, or lasso the grizzly with you. And more important, he will carry you home when you are too tired to walk." The tall man flipped Alvarado's feet up as if he were going to throw him off the fence backwards, but caught him at the last moment. They both laughed, and started for the *hacienda*.

"Do not listen to the chatter of the idle, *muchacho*," Ramon said. "You use those fine brown eyes, and watch, and learn, and believe what you see. Do not believe all the cackling of the barnyard birds." The old man ruffled the boy's hair.

The melody of the guitar wafted through the window. The soothing strains of the love song became the fast beating of a flamenco, and the dream changed.

The *fiesta* was crowded with *vaqueros* from *ranchos* miles away. The men were all in a field beyond the barns and corrals, while the women cooked and gossiped.

Proud Rancho Pornicula *vaqueros* bet all they had against equally proud *vaqueros* from other *ranchos.*

Chickens were buried up to their necks, and the men came at full gallop and bent far off their mounts, trying to pluck the heads from the birds.

They cut a steer from the herd, a steer with razor-sharp horns. They kept him separated, cutting him from the herd for a slow count of twenty-five. A rider worked his horse with his knees only, as the steer desperately tried to regain the safety of the group.

The *vaqueros* worked with their *reatas,* sixty-foot woven-leather ropes, and demonstrated the skills they'd acquired in their daily work.

The tall raw-boned palomino stallion that Ramon had so patiently trained was beneath the boy, but now did not turn his head to bite. He too wanted to take part in the competition.

The rodeo and *fiesta* had been going on for three days, and the boy had not yet gained the nerve to contest the men. He watched and learned and now sat on the tall palomino next to the *Segundo*, Ramon. Two older boys, boys who already were earning their way as *vaqueros*, reined up beside Alvarado and the *Segundo*, acting as if they were not there.

"Aw, but it is too bad the *fiesta* is almost concluded," one said to the other, purposefully loud. "I had hoped that the son of the *patrone* of La Pornicula . . . What is his name? Alvarado? I had hoped that he would instruct us in the ways of the *vaquero*. But I understand he has more important tasks. He oversees the kitchen, and the women. It is a very important job."

The two young *vaqueros* laughed. Quirting their horses, they rode to join the others. Their laughter made the hair bristle on the back of Alvarado's neck. Ramon understood, and tried to calm him. "There is plenty of time, *muchacho*. They are older and —"

Before Segundo could finish, Alvarado spurred the big stallion into a gallop and drew alongside the two young *vaqueros*. He reined the palomino to a sliding stop.

"That is a very fine head stall, and finely woven reins you have, Mariano," Alvarado said, addressing the taller and older of the two. "It would look much better on the head of a fine horse."

"The horse that wears it is the finest in all California, and his rider would wager it against any *muchacho* who thought he was a *vaquero*. But what would a *muchacho* wager?"

The fine bridle on Alvarado's palomino was given him by his father. It had silver *conchos* at the ear piece and bit, much finer than the one the young *vaquero* had. "Headstall for headstall," Alvarado answered, then immediately regretted his brashness. His father would not be pleased if the boy lost it. But he had little else to wager.

"And would the *muchacho* like to lose his fine headstall? Surely you would not care to race that bony, dirty-colored horse against mine. That would be unfair." The young man looked shrewdly at the boy, hoping against hope that he would gain the headstall by so easy a conquest. His bay stallion had never been beaten.

194

"What do you think, Sunfire?" Alvarado leaned forward and stroked the big palomino. "Do you wish to show this red horse your heels?"

Alvarado bit back the urge to decline the race. He had heard of the speed of the bay stallion, and had seen him carrying his rider earlier in the day. The bay was fast. Very fast. Instead Alvarado looked the *vaquero* directly in the eye. "Sunfire, says he has the time — just a little time — so he will make it very fast. What course do you suggest?"

A half mile across the cleared field, a giant live oak surveyed the headquarters of the *rancho*, as it had owned the land for four hundred years before the Cuens came. "Around that oak and back would be a fair distance. Do you need a head start?" The *vaquero* laughed and quirted the large red horse.

Alvarado dug his heels into the sides of the palomino and the horse almost leapt out from under him. The bay had a length head start, but that did not bother Alvarado so much as the glimpse he caught of his father reining up beside Ramon.

Then Alvarado was lost in his task. The pounding of the horses' hooves filled his ears. The bay was ahead but not gaining. Alvarado had never whipped the big palo-

195

mino, he'd never had to. But the tail of the looped lead rope which was bound to the saddle worked its way free and Alvarado grabbed it and brought it across the palomino's rump. The horse leapt forward, closing the gap.

They were neck and neck as they reached the oak. But the nimble *vaquero* made the turn much quicker than Alvarado and again he was a length behind.

Alvarado looked ahead and saw his father in the distance. He had been joined by most of the other guests who had gathered to watch the son of their host.

Alvarado could not lose this race.

Again he used the tail of the lead rope on the palomino, but it wasn't really necessary. The palomino was not one to lose. The horse sprang forward, chunks of earth flying from his hoofs, until he was neck and neck with the bay.

A hundred yards left. The *vaqueros* had lined the last forty yards and were waving their *sombreros,* encouraging the contestants. But not Lorenzo Cuen. The old man sat stoically on his mount, his hands folded on the saddle pommel, watching his only son.

The palomino leaped with renewed strength and pulled ahead. A half length. A length. Alvarado glanced back over his shoulder at the surprised young *vaquero.*

The *vaquero*'s eyes flared and he gritted his teeth. He was about to lose for the first time.

Suddenly Alvarado was sprawled spread-eagled in the dirt, the wind knocked from his aching chest, his *sombrero* torn from his neck and lying ten feet ahead in the dust. He'd blacked out, but couldn't have been unconscious for more than a few seconds. His father and the other men had not even reached him yet.

He'd let Sunfire down. The horse must have stepped in a squirrel hole — a hole Alvarado should have seen. Alvarado felt the wetness well up behind his eyes. Then he saw the big palomino.

The horse was standing, but had a foreleg raised.

Alvarado struggled to his feet and was at the palomino's side by the time the observers got to him. He quickly ran his hands over Sunfire's foreleg. No breaks. By the time his father and Ramon reached his side, the horse was placing his weight back on the forefoot. Alvarado sighed in relief.

His father placed his hands on the boy's shoulders. "Are you all right?"

Alvarado looked at the ground. "I am

sorry, Father. I lost."

"You won, Alvarado . . . at least in my eyes. You raced well. You lost the 'looking' contest. Next time miss the holes." Alvarado looked up to see his father was smiling. Alvarado grinned, then slipped the headstall off the roan and handed it to the young *vaquero.*

"We will race again, Mariano" he said smiling.

"As you wish, *señor*." The young man doffed his *sombrero,* spun the bay, and rode to where the Indians were ready to serve the Tule Elk that had been turning over oak coals all night.

Alvarado was secretly pleased. Not about the race, certainly not about losing the headstall. The man had not called him *muchacho.*

Don Alvarado Cuen awoke in deep darkness. The sounds of the twelve-string flamenco guitar still drifted into the open window of his room. He could hear laughter as the customers and girls passed by to find a place to consummate their transactions.

The music and laughter, and the dream, made him think of home. Home to him was still the Cuen Rancho — Rancho La Pornicula. The Ranch of the Laughing Waters.

Lorenzo's father, Alvarado's grandfather, had received the land grant for services to the crown just after the turn of the century. And after the old man died, Don Lorenzo Cuen had run the *rancho* well . . . at least until he failed to make a trip to re-establish his family grant after a fire destroyed the records in Monterey. The trip was long, and after all, everyone in California knew the Cuens. Rancho Pornicula belonged to them.

After the Bear Revolution, the *gringos* insisted that all land holdings be reconfirmed. The convention at Monterey, and the state's first constitution, maintained that Indians could not own land in California. Many part-Indian *mestizo* Mexicans walked away from land that had been in their families for generations.

Don Lorenzo had not left his land, and would not do so without a fight. But the new government wanted his ranch for an Indian reservation and Lorenzo could not prove title. With the help of two companies of dragoons the land was appropriated, and three generations of Cuen's were forced off — including twelve-year-old Alvarado.

Now, on a hill overlooking the abandoned effort at an Indian reservation, ten Cuen graves and the graves of the faithful who had worked the rancho sprouted weeds. The reservation had been a failure, but the land was sold by the state to a consortium from the East — not returned to the Cuens — and the proceeds went to the growing state's general fund.

Cuen could not help but remember the good times. The music and laughter wafting through the open window, and the dream, took him back — the *fandangos* and *fiestas*, the rodeos and roundups, thousands of cattle on fifteen thousand acres of golden, oak-covered land. It was never to be again. The land was still there, but the time was gone.

Cuen wished he could hate the *gringos*. He didn't. He hated the change, and the disappearance of the grizzly and the elk. He would no longer see herds of strong, pure Andalusian horses running free across the marshes of the central California valley. No more would the proud stallions be trained to perfection by equally proud *vaqueros* who would bet all they owned in rodeos against *vaqueros* from other *ranchos*. No more would brave *vaqueros* tallow their *reatas* so sharp claws could not drag man and horse to powerful jaws as they lassoed huge grizzlies for sport. No longer would the Tule Elk roast over huge fires. The meat-hunters supplying the gold fields had just about wiped out the big bears and the elk.

A time was passing, and Alvarado Cuen hated it. But not so much as he hated the fact that his father, his proud father, who loved Rancho Pornicula more than life itself, was buried behind Tia Carlita's whorehouse.

Alvarado's thoughts were interrupted by the creaking of the door. He caught the scent of rose water, and watched in the faint moonlight that caressed the room, as a slender girl slipped out of her blouse and long full skirt. She slid expertly into the bed beside him. The warmth of her body was not uncomfortable, even in the heat of the July night.

Her tongue tasted his neck and she nibbled at his ear until he rolled to face her. He wrapped his hand around the small of her back and pulled her tight against him.

She whispered in his ear, as his manhood rose to the occasion, "It is Chapa, Don Alvarado. I have come to please you."

"It would please me if you would call me Al, and if you locked the door."

For the next hour, he forgot the throbbing in his head.

CHAPTER FOURTEEN

Ned studied the schedule the City Council had delivered to his office. This was Thursday the second of July. The Fourth of July festivities would begin with a dance and box social on Friday the third. They would continue on Saturday the fourth with a picnic and baseball game, and conclude with a dance and fireworks on Saturday night.

Today he would be expected to work the streets. The Fourth of July was about the biggest celebration of the year, and one of the rowdiest. Now that the sentiments of the War Between the States were finally settling down, the fistfight would be limited to drunks no longer motivated by North and South sympathies as they had been when Ned was growing up. He remembered how rough some of those fights had been. Some had even ended in gunplay.

One thing the weekend would not be was

quiet. The Chinese loved their fireworks and, on Saturday, the Tenderloin would resemble the Battle of Gettysburg. The organized city-sponsored fireworks would be dwarfed by the usually staid and conservative Chinese. If the South had created as much noise as the Chinese would on Saturday, the war might have ended differently.

The volunteer fire department would have a busy day just putting out brush and grass fires. Ned and Theo would have at least three runaway horses, ten fistfights, and twenty drunks to deal with.

Ned was trying to decide if he needed to deputize a couple more fellows for part-time on the weekend, when Ratzlaff and a short, stocky man crashed into the office.

Theo was red-faced and his jaw was tightly set. The stocky fellow's ashen white face contrasted with his curly black hair.

Ratzlaff went into the back room, returned with a cup of coffee, and handed it to the man. Then he turned to Ned. "This is Juan Etcheverry. Juan runs sheep up in the hills on the other side of the river. Tell him what you tol' me, Juan."

The man was visibly shaken as he walked to Ned's desk and set the coffee cup down. "The man at ferry. Mr. Max. He has been killed. I have to swim across this morning."

"Killed. How?" Ned was on his feet.

The man ran a finger across his throat. "Very bad. A trail from his shack in to the brush. So much blood. Like someone butchered the hog." He shook his head and walked over to sit on the bench near the window.

Ned grabbed the .44 from the coat tree and strapped it on. "That's in the county. Theo, you go an' tell the Sheriff. I'm gonna' get on out there."

"He was a friend of mine too, Ned. I'm going with you. Mr. Etcheverry, would you mind going on over to the Sheriff's office in the county courthouse and telling them what happened?"

"Yes, yes, I will do that. Then I must get back to my sheep. I have been gone too long now." The Basque returned to the desk and gulped down the coffee, then followed Ned and Theo out the door.

Cody and Ratzlaff hurried to the livery, then loped their horses the three miles to Gordon's Ferry.

Max's body lay crumpled in the brush, not fifty feet from the front door of the shack. It was not difficult to find. A splattered trail of blood pointed the way. Old Maxwell Twill had put up a fight. The inside of the shack was a mess. Table and chairs were upended, the cast-iron stove was knocked off its brick base and its stack knocked askew. Black soot mixed with the pool of blood on the floor, contrasting with the drying blood that splattered the walls.

They looked carefully over the scene without comment. Ned studied the floor, then walked beside the trail to the body. Already the flies had begun their work in the morning sun. When he returned to the shack, Ned's stomach churned and he felt nauseated. But concentrating on the job at hand, he turned his nausea to steely resolve.

Finally, Ned grabbed a blanket and threw it to Theo. "Cover him up," Cody said. The big deputy tossed it back to him.

"Would you mind, Ned? Old Max was a friend of mine. This makes me sick." Theo turned and walked on out to the riverside and sat on a log, watching the peaceful water glide by.

Ned placed the blanket carefully over the old man. Not only was Max's throat slashed, but his hands were badly cut. Obviously he had tried to fend off his attacker.

As Ned studied the sign and returned again to the cabin, Puttyworth and Winston rode up, reining their horses near the shack. George Howard was close behind in a buggy. The two deputies stomped into the shack, looked around, then followed the trail to the body. "God damn," Ned heard Putty-worth mumble, as they stomped back over the trail, obliterating any prints that they might have investigated.

Ned walked to his horse. Gathering up his reins, he led his and Theo's horse to where the big deputy sat. "Let's go on, Theo. I've seen enough."

George Howard clambered down from the buggy as they passed. "You boys are a little out of your territory, ain't you?" The big man stood with thumbs hooked into his belt.

"It's all yours, Sheriff." Ned came as close to ignoring him as he could, but Theo reined his gray over close to Howard and bent down.

"That man was an old friend of mine," Theo hissed. "You fellows take good care to see that what's left of him is treated respect-fully. I'll send the digger out to get him." He reined the gray away and caught up with the departing Ned.

"Humph," the Sheriff grunted, not think-ing it wise to say more to the very large, very serious city deputy.

As they plodded up China Grade, Ratzlaff rode up beside Ned. "What do you think? You got any ideas?"

"I don't know who, Theo," Cody answered, "but I know one thing. Fella who did that has been around town for a few days, and is probably riding a buckskin horse. And is probably John Tenkiller."

"How do you figger?"

"Same boot tracks as at Gum San's. A nick on the heel of the left boot. Plain as day in all that soot and Max's drying blood."

They rode on in silence.

Ricardo Urrea awoke with mixed emotions.

John Tenkiller had returned, riled and unhappy, complaining about being broke. But the half-breed wasn't so unhappy that he didn't stay busy in the next room with the sisters. Ricardo worried about what the Sheriff really had in mind for them. Urrea feared Tenkiller, but he feared the Sheriff also.

Tenkiller interrupted his thoughts by sticking his pock-marked face into the brothers' room. "You two rustle up some coffee and grub," he growled. "I got a hunger that's only half satisfied." Ricardo poked his brother, who still slept. Enrico rubbed his eyes, saw Tenkiller, and furrowed his brows but said nothing.

"Pull on your clothes, Enrico," Ricardo ordered, hurrying his brother along. "Johnny wants some coffee. Get some of Maria's sweetbread."

Johnny had started to close the door to return to the girls when Ricardo stopped him. "Johnny," he whispered, "get your breeches on. There's something in the cellar I want to show you."

Tenkiller looked over his shoulder a little suspiciously, then nodded and went for his clothes. The pockets of his trousers did not jingle as he wished. The old man had had only a few dimes in the box and nothing else of value. Johnny decided he would wait until Cordova's pockets and cash box were full, then put his stubby revolver in the Mexican's belly and relieve him of his gold. Only then would Tenkiller leave town.

Johnny watched as Ricardo got a candle from the top of a bureau, then followed him silently down the stairs that led to the cellar. Johnny had been down there once before, but other than the Chinese who lolled in the Room of Heavenly Pleasures, he'd found little of interest. Ricardo did not enter that room, however. He went, instead, into the center room — a musty storeroom, stuffed to the brim with rat-eaten furniture.

"What are you showing me, Ricardo? A lot of junk?"

"No, Johnny, something very valuable."

Ricardo walked to the back and pulled a tall chair to the side, then tore away an old, heavy sheet-metal sign. "Come here. Look."

Johnny was still a little suspicious, but came forward. There was an eighteen-inch-wide-by-four-foot-high opening in the brick wall of the cellar.

Ricardo thrust the candle into the hole revealing a large tunnel. Timbers strengthened the dirt walls. A large rat scampered away from the candlelight.

"Where does it go, Ricardo?" Johnny asked.

"Did you see the ruins of the building?" Urrea pointed to the north.

Johnny had noticed the burnt-out remains of a building during his wanderings. Most of the building had collapsed into the cellar and little was left. It was a hundred or more good paces north of Charley Bok Yue's and away from any other structures.

"I saw it. The tunnel goes there?"

"Yes, and it is open and clear all the way. It makes two turns, but is easy to follow."

Johnny smiled, the first Ricardo had seen since the one that crossed his pock-marked face when Tenkiller had first met the sisters. Johnny placed his hand on Ricardo's shoulder. "This is good. Very good, *amigo.*"

Ricardo spoke in his most sincere tone.

"Johnny, you know if they come — the law, I mean — Enrico and I will help you. You are our good friend."

"Bueno, amigo." Johnny answered, but looked at his "friend" with skepticism.

CHAPTER FIFTEEN

Mary Beth loved the yellow, white-trimmed house her father had built. Her only regret was that her mother had not lived to enjoy it more. The house was a half mile out of town to the west, on Nineteenth Street. There was only an acre of land, but that was as her father had wished. The only out building was a carriage house. The gazebo next to the house, open on all sides and covered with wisteria, could not really be considered a building.

Mary Beth sat on the canopied bed in her room on the second floor and carefully unwrapped the box that her stepmother Frances had sent down on the train. The organdy dress was breathtaking. The note lying in the box on top of the dress was Frances's way of letting her stepdaughter know what she was missing.

Mary Beth:

Wish you were here. There are so many beautiful gowns but I am afraid to buy them without a proper fitting. As you can see, the styles have changed and we'll have to throw out all your old things.

Father had a wonderful welcome party for us, with lots of handsome, very rich, young men.

So sorry you could not be with me. They were all disappointed. Wish you were here.

Love, Frances

Mary Beth held the dress up in front of her, studying it in the mirror on the armoire. It was organdy silk with a slightly darker embroidered trim. The embroidery ran in two rows from the high regal neckline, curving from the outside of the neckline to the center of the bodice, then to the waist. There was no bustle. Instead it fit snugly over the hips down to the top of the thighs, only then flaring slightly. The hem just barely touched the floor. The box also contained a matching hat, parasol, and soft kid slippers. With the tight-fitting bodice and the hip-hugging skirt, the dress would show off her figure far more than the bustled dresses that filled her closet and armoire. She loved the dress, but wondered if her father would approve.

If her stepmother knew one thing, it was how to dress. Mary Beth had a twinge of guilt that she'd not accompanied her step-mother, and a twinge of envy that Frances was there and she was not. Then she thought of the box social and wondered if the dress was too nice for the occasion. All the women would be dressed well, but not *this* well. She decided to try it on.

Mary Beth slipped out of her nightgown, standing naked for a moment. Then she decided it would not be proper without the corset, even though she didn't actually need one. She went through the whole process of dressing, despite the fact that the box social didn't start until seven and she would have to dress all over again. Mary Beth just had to know if it fit. How she looked would help her box dinner bring a higher price. She hoped that buyer would be Ned Cody.

After a few minutes, she undressed, hung up the organdy, and pulled on a simple gingham dress in which to ride to town. Mary Beth still needed the makings of a scrumptious dinner and a basket to pack it in.

She stuck her head out the upstairs window and called out to the man who kept the grounds when not involved with odd jobs around Nelson's office, "Pedro, would you please hitch up the buggy?"

Two Chinese worked atop the carriage-house roof. With a bundle of shingles and hammers, they tat-tatted while chattering away.

Mary Beth was in a wonderful mood. Her twinges of envy and guilt had completely passed. She waved merrily at the workers on the roof as she climbed in the carriage. As they politely stood on the steep roof and bowed their heads, one slipped, barely managing to grab the ridge and halt a slide that would have dumped him ten feet to the ground. Mary Beth gasped, then let her breath out when she realized he would be all right.

The Chinese were too polite for their own good, she decided.

Ned Cody sensed that John Tenkiller was in town. Both crimes that he'd attributed to the half-breed were committed close to the city.

He wanted this man, wanted him more than anything he had ever wanted.

It was becoming an obsession.

As much as he looked forward to the

picnic with Mary Beth, he almost wished that he didn't have the commitment. The celebration just might bring the man out onto the streets.

If he was here.

Tenkiller could have hightailed it out of town after he killed the old man. Any sane man wouldn't have killed old Maxwell Twill in the first place. Which reminded Ned that he had to be at Max's funeral at two this afternoon.

Yes, it made sense that John Tenkiller would light a shuck, but somehow Ned felt the man was still close by. The thought frustrated him.

Why would a desert Indian from Arizona come to Bakersfield? Why would Sheriff Potter think the man was on his way here to begin with? Ned chastised himself. He should have wired the Wyoming Sheriff for more information days ago.

Cody decided that he would walk the Tenderloin again and talk to whomever he could. Right now, talk seemed his only weapon.

Sticking his head in Callahan's, Ned noticed Nelly and Jimmy "One Eye." He walked to the bar and again showed them the poster he carried folded in his shirt pocket, but they assured him that they had seen no one as mean-looking as John Ten-killer. Sill's and White's had a few cowhands at the bar. The town was starting to fill up with range hands and miners. Some had ridden for two or three days to be part of the Independence celebration.

Again he got nowhere. He stopped in three other places before he got to Cordova's.

Hector Cordova sat at his usual table, sipping a beer. A Mexican worked the faro table dealing to two cowhands who looked as if they were already behind the sixes. Another Mexican worked the bar. A small, black-eyed, raven-haired bar girl in a scarlet dress and black knit stockings stood talking with two tough-looking Mexican miners. Ned walked straight to Cordova's table.

Cody knew the man slightly, but Cordova was the only one in the saloon that he did know. Ned eyed the faro table as he passed, and caught the dealer looking up. The man's eyes noticeably flared and he quickly looked back to his game. Sometimes the badge had that effect, but Ned wondered.

He turned his attention to the owner.

"Mr. Cordova. Can I join you a minute?" Not waiting for an answer, Ned pulled a chair.

"Marshal." Cordova nodded, motioning

him to the chair he was already taking. Then he waved the bar girl over.

"You want a beer, Cody?"

"No. No, thanks. I got a big weekend ahead." Ned unfolded the poster and pushed it across the table.

"*Si,*" Hector said, pushing it back. "We got the one you put up over there." He pointed to the back door.

"I'm still lookin' for him. And I want him! You mind if I show it around the bar?" Ned stood, preparing to pass it around no matter what the man's answer.

"No problem, Cody."

"You seen him?" Ned wondered if the whole Mexican community would take the same attitude as Al Cuen. The "blood of my blood" attitude.

"No, Cody. If I had, I'd come runnin'. We don't need the like of him around."

"Thanks, Cordova. You keep an eye peeled." Ned walked to the bar and motioned to the tall Mexican bartender.

"Beer?" the man asked coolly.

"No. Information. You seen this man?" Ned pushed the poster across the bar.

"Never heard of him. You want a beer?" Enrico stepped on down the bar and poured a couple more for the miners.

"No. I want this man."

The bartender shrugged his shoulders and ignored Cody. Irritated, Ned turned and walked to the faro table.

He stood behind the players, and again the chubby Mexican noticeably winced when he saw Cody.

"Don't mean to interrupt the game, boys. But have any of you fellas seen this man?" Ned threw the poster out onto the center of the table. A cowhand turned the poster so it was right side up to him, and studied it for a moment. "I saw a fellow looked a little like this. Passed him on the trail comin' down from Lorraine wearin' a fancy *sombrero* and totin' two pearl-handled colts. Had a new 73 Winchester in the saddle scabbard and another short-barrel carbine across the back of his saddle."

"Buckskin horse?" Ned asked excitedly.

"Na, biggest black stallion that you ever saw. Silver-studded saddle. That boy didn't have no scars that you'd notice, though."

"Was he comin' or goin'?" Ned pressed, now sure that the helpful cowboy had the wrong man.

"Goin'."

Ned spun the poster to the dealer. "How about you? You dealt any cards to this man?" Noticeably nervous, the dealer dealt the next card off the table onto the floor, then knocked over a beer as he scrambled to retrieve it.

"No, *señor*. I have seen no one." Ricardo got up and left the table, crossing to the bar for a towel. Ned waited patiently.

"You sure, *señor*?" Ned's tone hardened as he narrowed his eyes and studied the chubby dealer.

"Never have I seen such a man." Ricardo's tone was almost pleading. Ned noticed that the man had never once looked at him. He was sure the dealer was either lying or a wanted man himself. Getting nowhere with the questioning, Ned stood up and walked back to Cordova's table.

"Hector, how long you had that dealer workin' here?"

"A couple of years, Cody. You've seen him before. He's right enough. He sure as hell ain't your man."

"It's not that. He's just nervous as hell."

"That badge makes folks nervous, Cody, case you haven't noticed." Hector Cordova smiled. "Sure you won't have a beer? It's on the house."

"No. Thanks, Hector. Another time." Ned turned and started for the door. He hesitated, then walked back.

"Where does that boy hang his hat at

night?" he said, motioning towards the faro table.

"Charley Good Book's, Ned. But he's not your man."

"Don't doubt that, Hector. Thanks."

The walk to Charley's was short. Ned chastised himself for not talking to Charley earlier. Charley knew as much about the Tenderloin as anyone — maybe more.

But would Charley tell him anything?

Johnny paced the room like a caged cat.

He had to get out of this place. The only thing holding him back was money. He would have shoved the stubby .450 in Cordova's ribs and been long gone last night, had Ricardo not innocently given him a most valuable piece of information. Saturday was one of the biggest days of the year for the saloon. The money box would be stuffed full when they closed on Saturday night. Johnny could wait. It was only one more day.

Still, he was very nervous. For the hundredth time, he walked to the window, then stopped short. Looking across the street, Johnny recognized the tall man with the big colt hung butt forward. The Marshal was coming towards the boardinghouse with the purposeful stride of a man who knew where he was going.

Johnny pulled the window open and grabbed his Henry rifle. He stood back in the shadow of the room, taking a careful bead on the metal star on the tall man's chest reflecting the noon light.

Tenkiller watched as the man crossed the street. Then a buggy reined up between Johnny and the man with the badge.

It was the same girl. The most beautiful girl Tenkiller had ever seen. She laughed and spoke to the tall man, and he smiled back at her. Johnny wished he could hear what they were saying.

The girl waved and moved her team off. Johnny lowered the rifle and slipped it under the bed, quickly running for the back stairs and down to the street level.

Clattering through the boxes and barrels that littered the rear yard, and across the rear yards of the next buildings, Johnny followed the same direction the girl had taken. Two blocks to the west he saw the buggy tied in front of a dry-goods store.

Johnny stepped into the shadow of a doorway and waited.

CHAPTER SIXTEEN

Ned felt a strange chill when he walked through the ornately carved gate in front of Charley's. He had experienced the same feeling ever since he was a boy. Ned never knew what caused it. Perhaps it was the evil-looking wooden dogs guarding each side. Perhaps it was the incongruous crucified Jesus hanging by the front door. Or maybe it was the strange Buddha he knew rested in the cellar — or the habits of the inhabitants of the "room of heavenly pleasure" at the other end of the cellar.

Cody shook off the feeling and climbed the porch stairs two at a time. Before he went inside, Ned slipped the thong off the hammer of his Colt.

He climbed the narrow stairs off the front hall to the second floor, then rapped on Charley's door. A door behind him creaked open and an overly made-up Chinese lady peeked out. Seeing Cody, she quietly disappeared back into her room.

Charley Good Book's door opened a crack, then swung wide. Charley stood there, clutching a Bible to his bulging belly, and bowed his head politely. "Marsh' Cody, you honor my humble home."

Ned stepped inside. He'd never been in Charley's room before and was amazed at the opulent furnishings. He studied the furniture, carpets, and wall coverings in silence.

"Would you care for tea?" Charley asked politely. It was already so hot in the room that the sweat was running from under Cody's hat band and dripping onto his collar. "No, Charley. Thank you. Just a couple of questions." Charley smiled and nodded.

"You got a boarder here, fellow that deals faro at Cordova's?"

"Yes, Marsh' Ned. Has he done something?" Charley asked, laying the Bible aside.

"No. At least not that I know of. I'm just curious." Ned dug the folded poster out of his shirt pocket and handed it to Charley. The Chinaman's fat fingers fumbled with it until he finally got it unfolded. "You seen that fella around?" Ned asked, studying Charley's expression carefully. But the man indicated nothing more than sincere concern.

"No, Marsh' Cody. I never see this man."

"Would you mind lettin' me into this dealer's room?"

"It my honor to be of service." Charley crossed to an intricately carved table. Carefully, so as not to upset the tall painted vase that rested on top, he pulled open a small drawer and sorted through the mass of keys it contained.

"He does not stay alone, Marsh' Cody. His brother in the room with him. And sisters share next room."

"Are they there now?"

"I do not know, Marsh'. But we see." Deftly negotiating his way through the door into the hall, Charles crossed to the Urreas' room. He rapped on the door and received no answer. He turned the key in the lock.

Resting a hand on the butt of his Colt, Cody stepped inside. Charley mumbled behind him, "I leave you to your work. Please to tell me when you leave, so I can lock door." With that, the fat man hurried back to his room.

Ned searched the surroundings, then tried the unlocked connecting door. He scoured the second room as well, going through each drawer carefully until satisfied that nothing was amiss. A tin box rested on top of a bureau. Ned found something vaguely familiar about the container, but soon dismissed the thought. The sweets the box contained meant nothing to Cody. One pair of boots lay under the bed and he reached down and pulled them out. The heel was not cut. He positioned the boots the way he had found them but searched no further under the bed.

Stopping his search short of complete, Ned yelled to Charley through the door, then hurried to the livery. He would have to take the roan to Union Cemetery and Max's funeral. It was too far to walk.

Johnny did not like waiting in the doorway even though it was deep, shaded, and dark. He felt the look of every passerby and pulled the brim of his hat low over his eyes, tucking in his chin.

Finally he heard laughter. The girl was saying something to a clerk who carried her package to the buggy. Johnny stepped forward, watching intently as she tut-tutted at the bay horse and reined around the next corner.

Johnny was wary. He had never been this far into town, nor this far away from the Tenderloin. Crossing the wide main street, he followed an alley paralleling the route the girl had taken. He trotted along, catching an occasional glimpse of her moving the buggy down the street.

He came to a vacant lot, and waited for her to pass. Several seconds went by. Cursing under his breath for waiting too long, Johnny crossed the lot to the street. The buggy was tied up in front of a grocery.

Tenkiller hid behind two tall, full, oleander bushes, not noticing their white and red blossoms. He had eyes only for the buggy . . . and for its driver.

The girl came out and again her laughter could be heard as she chatted merrily with a Chinese boy who placed her packages behind the buggy seat.

Johnny stepped deeper behind the bushes as she passed. Watching the pale, creamy-complected beauty, Tenkiller licked his lips. The girl's long blond hair fell almost to her waist and her blue eyes sparkled. She sang to herself, her voice carrying over the clattering hooves of the bay mare she was driving.

The buggy cleared the last of the houses at the edge of town, and drove on. Johnny now wished he had the buckskin. Without the horse, he would either have to run to catch up with her or let her go. Then he spotted the big yellow house in the distance.

He worked his way along a ravine which paralleled the road fifty yards to its north, through a field covered with sage and buck brush. Pulling off his boots and carrying them, Johnny trotted barefoot. The trotting did not tire him. He could run fifty miles in the desert sun and had done so many times before as a young brave in Arizona.

Finally, his persistence was rewarded. The girl pulled the buggy up to an outbuilding behind the yellow house. A Mexican ran over and helped her down, then took the packages from the back of the buggy and followed her inside.

Johnny worked his way through the scrub brush, glancing occasionally at the house, until he faced it from the west. The shadow of a red-tailed hawk startled him. He looked up, admiring the hunting raptor, feeling a primeval affinity for the predatory. Then once again, he focused his full attention on the house.

The Mexican was in the rear yard, working at a flower bed. The only other sign of life was two Chinese workmen, pounding away at the roof of an outbuilding.

Johnny carefully made his way from the scrub, over a short rail fence into the manicured grounds, then to a vine-covered frame that rose beside the house. Carefully, he kept the vine between him and the workers.

There was no sign of movement in any of the windows. No horses or wagons were in sight. Could he be so lucky as to have found her in the house alone?

Johnny considered coming back at night. But the chances of her being alone then would be less than in the afternoon. The man of the house would be returning at night.

While the workers concentrated on their job, Johnny slipped, as quiet as the shadow of the hawk circling overhead, to the front of the building. He worked his way through the shrubs to the front porch. Seldom had Johnny seen a house as grand as this one. He was pleased that the steps did not creak as he padded softly to the front door.

Two beveled-glass side panels lined the jambs of the door. Shading his eyes from the reflecting sun, he gazed inside.

Mary Beth was whistling and singing as she unpacked the wrapped groceries. She had been able to find fresh berries and was particularly pleased. Mary Beth knew her mother had left her a grand legacy — the ability to make the best pie crust in creation. If the bidders at the box social weren't impressed by a fresh berry pie, then nothing would impress them. She spread flour on the metal shelf of the pie safe, grabbed a bowl and a wooden spoon, and fetched a small wooden tub of lard. Carefully, she spooned four large measures of lard into the bowl. She thought she heard something in the entry.

The door squeaked.

Could it be that her father was home this early?

She wiped her hands on her apron and started for the front parlor.

Then she heard the scream.

She knocked over some flour as she ran for the rear yard. The wooden tub of lard tumbled off the shelf and came crashing to the floor.

Pedro was hurrying across the grass toward the carriage house. One Chinese worker was climbing down from the roof. Mary Beth could not see the other at first.

The second man was lying where he had fallen, his face grimacing in pain. His forearm was broken and bulging as bone pushed against flesh. Mary Beth dropped to her knees beside him, tenderly inspecting the damaged arm. She directed Pedro to bring one of the shingles from the pile that had fallen with the man. Breaking it in half the long way, across her knee, she splinted the Chinaman's arm. She bound the shingles tightly with her apron. The man winced.

"Help him into the buggy, Pedro," Mary Beth said firmly. "I'll drive him to Doc Gilroy's. That arm's got to be set."

"I can drive him, *señorita,*" Pedro offered.

Mary Beth hesitated. She had so much to do before the box social and if she didn't get the pie started, there would be no pie tonight. She signed and nodded to him to go ahead, and started back to the kitchen and the pie dough.

Then she stopped and turned.

No. The man was in pain, and Mary Beth was responsible for anyone who worked at the house when her father was not there. Box social or no, pie or no pie. Ned Cody — or whoever — would have to make do with what she could whip up later. It would be irresponsible to let someone else handle the problem.

"Bring the buggy over, Pedro. I'll take him," she said, thinking that she would simply have to rely on the organdy dress to entice the bidders.

Johnny watched from the kitchen window as the man was loaded into the buggy. He cursed to himself as the girl climbed into the seat and reined away.

He grabbed a handful of berries and began looking through the house for something he might take.

Maybe she would be back.

CHAPTER SEVENTEEN

Ned reined the roan up in front of his office, loosened the cinch, and walked him around to the alley where the big horse could wait in the shade. As he walked to the office door, he thought about how temporary life was.

The funeral had been a small one. There hadn't been a lot of time to let people know. It was too hot to keep a man waiting long to be planted. The minister hadn't known Max well since old Max had seldom come to town. He'd worked the ferry seven days a week, including Sunday, so other folks could make it to church.

The eulogy was short and sweet, which raised no complaint from anyone — it was damn hot under the treeless bone-orchard sun. The minister said a few words about how hard old Max had worked, about how good he was to the kids, giving them candy and tying their fish hooks and digging bait for them, and how Max would get his rest in the next world. Then it was ashes to ashes, dust to dust, the Lord's Prayer, and they all threw a handful of dirt into the hole and left the rest of it to the digger.

Ned took the time to walk over to where his folks were buried. He didn't say a silent prayer, but silently asked his old man how to get the son of a bitch who had killed Max after paying a visit to Ling Su's chicken house.

But Ned received no answer.

Cody made a mental note to come back out and hoe the weeds around his parents' headstone when he had the time and when the working weather was better.

Lost in thoughts of his father, he rode back to the office. Something was troubling him. Something that he had missed.

There was a note pinned to his office door. It was short and to the point. "Sheriff wants to see you."

Cody had just about made up his mind the last time he was at George Howard's office that, if the fat Sheriff wanted to see him, he could come to the City Marshal's office. But Ned wanted this John Tenkiller, wanted him bad. And he was ready to deal with the devil if that was what it took to get the murderer. Maybe that was what the note was all about.

Ned walked the four blocks to the county courthouse.

Puttyworth and Winston were lounging around in Cap Colston's outer office. They barely looked up as Ned entered. The visored Colston got up and walked into Howard's inner office, then returned almost immediately and motioned Cody on in.

Howard was sitting at his desk, gnawing on a cigar and studying a batch of papers. Ned grabbed a ladder-backed chair, spun it around, and straddled it backwards, facing the Sheriff. "What's up, Howard?" he asked.

Howard turned on his swivel chair and surveyed Cody. "Have a seat, Marshal," he sneered, his tone more sarcastic than usual.

Ned stood and moved the chair aside.

Howard looked up at him and furrowed his brow. "You change your mind about workin' with us? This is the last time I'm gonna ask."

At first Ned was incredulous that the man doubted his last word on the subject. Then his disbelief turned to anger. The heat rose in the back of his neck. The Sheriff pressed on.

"Puttyworth and Winston jus' came from Goetting's place. He's gonna be open in time for the big doin's tomorrow. He's

234

willin' to up the percentage to ten. We only been charging him seven, so you are in for three. And there's all the other saloons in the city." Howard raised his eyebrows, awaiting an answer.

Ned stared into Howard's pig eyes. The fat bastard had gone to Goetting again, after Ned had assured the saloon keeper that he would have to pay nothing but taxes to do business in the city. Goetting must be thinking Ned was a real fool.

Cody placed a booted foot on the seat of Howard's swivel chair, between the man's fat knees, and shoved.

The chair careened the six feet to the wall. Howard opened his mouth, dropping his lighted cigar in his lap, as he slammed against the wall. The whole room shook.

The Sheriff tried to rise, but Cody was on him in an instant. Grabbing Howard's collar with his left hand and shaking his right fist in Howard's face, Ned screamed, "You fat son of a bitch! I told you to stay away from the folks who live in the city! You spread your pig shit in the county! While you can!"

Howard's face reddened. He tried to stand and hook an overhand right to Cody's extended left arm. Cody ducked under it and spun the big man by the collar.

235

George Howard crashed to the floor over his swivel chair just as Puttyworth, with Winston at his heels, ran into the office.

Puttyworth reached for the Colt at his hip. Before he cleared leather, Ned had Puttyworth by the collar. He cocked his .44 and jammed it under Puttyworth's chin.

"And I've had about enough of you two. I'm tellin' all you county boys. Don't you come into the city for anything other than to pick up your laundry."

Winston had his hand on the butt of his holstered Colt. Ned locked gazes with him and jammed the big .44 deeper into the soft underside of Puttyworth's chin, driving the deputy to his toes and tilting his head back.

Ned spoke with quiet earnest to Winston. "You pull that and your eyes will be full of this donkey's brains before you clear leather." When the man moved his hand from the Colt, Ned shoved Puttyworth away. "Now both you boys two-finger that iron out onto the floor."

Ned reached for George Howard's gun belt, which hung on a peg on the wall. Howard was still on the floor, watching carefully, his face red and eyes bulging with hate.

The deputies carefully dropped their guns. Ned motioned them back to the wall. He bent and gathered both Colts, draping Howard's gun belt over his forearm. Then he casually flipped the deputies' guns through George Howard's favorite tall window. The glass exploded with a crashing tinkle. Still on the floor, Howard quickly scrambled clear of the falling shards.

Through the now-gaping open window, Ned tossed Howard's gun, belt and all, out into the street. Then he walked to the door. "You boys take care of the county, at least as long as you got your jobs. The next time I see you, you better have a smile on your faces and your hands clear of anything you might be carryin'."

As Marshal Ned Cody walked through the outer office, a wide-eyed Cap Colston scrambled out the door, his green visor askew on his forehead. By the time Ned reached the street, Colston was nowhere in sight.

Inside the Sheriff's office, Winston and Puttyworth moved quickly to the rack of long guns on the wall. Puttyworth grabbed a scattergun, and Winston a 73 Winchester. George Howard climbed back to his feet. "You boys jus' leave those be," he said quietly, his eyes dark and menacing. "You'll have your chance soon enough."

Ned Cody stomped across Railroad Avenue. His bristles were up. Those sons of bitches had been asking for their come-uppance for as long as Ned had known them. Cody was glad it had finally taken place.

The problem now was trying to do his job without the cooperation of the Sheriff's office. He knew any relationship with Howard was over. But Ned had already chosen the trail he'd ride. He'd place the matter of the Sheriff's charging for "protection" in front of the County Board of Supervisors.

Ned had never underestimated Sheriff George Howard. The man was a cunning politician. What relationship the Sheriff had with and what favors were owed him by the individual members of the Board of Supervisors remained to be seen. If the Board didn't throw Howard out, Cody knew he was in for a long few months until the next election. If Howard didn't lose the election, Cody was in for a long four years. Still, he decided as he reached his office, he wasn't sorry he'd cut his wolf loose. It was long overdue.

Each time Ling Su cried out in the night, Toothless Gum San Choy felt himself getting angry all over again. He was angry at the man who'd hurt her. He was angry at

238

all the whites, and the browns, because they'd spawned such a man. He was angry at his Chinese brethren because they had not spotted the rapist and come to tell him. If they had, he didn't know if he would have taken the matter to Marsh' Ned, or if he would have used his own tong hatchet to make sure the monster never dishonored another young girl.

Above all, he was angry at himself for not having heard what was happening in the chicken house and rushing to his daughter's aid.

He didn't know what he would do if a little brown devil grew inside his young daughter. He guessed he would pray to all the gods that it had almond eyes, and straight black hair, and skin the beautiful color of the litchi nut.

All day Toothless had walked the streets of the Tenderloin. He'd worked each of the saloons, refilling crocks with Ling Su's pickled eggs, taking more time than usual to eye each patron carefully. It was very difficult. They all looked alike to him.

He'd talked to every Chinese he knew, and some he didn't know, asking about the man with the sallow, thin face and the cut boot heel. Most looked at Toothless as if he had left his good sense behind in the Province

239

of Jiangsu. They seldom investigated the heels of men's boots while conducting business. Still Toothless pressed on. Vengeance would be his, he decided. It was the only thing that would abate his anger.

Toothless was tired and his feet ached from his rounds. Tomorrow he would take some time for himself, allowing himself the pleasure of Gi Lu's ministrations. She would soothe his aching muscles, and his aching mind.

The doctor was not in his office when Mary Beth arrived with the Chinese workman in tow. Mary Beth watched the injured man grimace each time he moved. Taking pity on him, she walked to a nearby Chinese shop and purchased a bottle of rice wine. The man's eyes lit up when she returned. And by the time Doctor Gilroy arrived, the workman was much more relaxed and happy and numb . . .

The sandy-haired doctor went to work immediately. Mary Beth admired the skill with which he operated. She'd said hello to Gilroy at church, but that was the only time she'd had occasion to chat with him.

"This is a wonderful job of stabilizing," the handsome young doctor said as he removed the apron which tied up the wounded man's splinted arm. "Did you do this?"

"Why, yes, thank you," Mary Beth replied, flipping a stray lock of long blond hair off her shoulder. "I thought it would hurt less if it didn't move."

"Well, you were exactly right." The man winced as the doctor carefully straightened the arm at the elbow above the break. "Help me here a moment." He smiled at Mary Beth, motioning her towards the table. He handed the bottle to the Chinaman. "You take another swig of this." The workman quickly drained the last of it.

"Get this shirt off," the doctor directed at Mary Beth. She removed it as carefully as possible. The break was pressing at the surface, looking as if the bone would pierce the skin with the slightest movement.

The doctor folded the man's good arm across his chest. "You put all your weight on his good arm," he said, "and hold him down. I'm going to have to give his arm a pull to align the bone."

Mary Beth felt apprehensive, but she had come this far and she would see it through. The injured man's eyes widened. He muttered something in Chinese as the doctor extended his broken arm out to the side and placed a foot in the patient's armpit. Mary

241

Beth rested all her weight on the good arm, pinning it to the Chinaman's chest. Doctor Gilroy jerked quickly.

Mary Beth could hear the bone grind as it seated itself. The patient didn't complain, and Mary Beth suddenly realized why. He'd passed out cold.

She straightened up, feeling somewhat nauseous, the color draining from her face. The doctor quickly made his way around the table, but Mary Beth made no effort to speak. The room spun and she suddenly felt weak in the knees.

The doctor caught her before she hit the ground and helped her to a chair.

"Thank you for your help," he said to her, softly. "You did very well."

Mary Beth's head began to clear, but she still felt a bit queasy. "I . . . I was afraid I was going to add to the problem for a moment, Dr. Gilroy."

"How about you calling me Tom," he said, flashing her a broad grin.

"Thank you, Tom." Mary Beth returned his smile. "Could I have a glass of water?"

The doctor grabbed a glass and poured her a drink from a bone-white pitcher. "You'll be fine in a second," he assured her. "Are you going to the box social tonight?"

"Why yes," Mary Beth replied, a bit

surprised by the abrupt turn in the conversation. As she drank, the doctor walked back to his now-stirring patient.

"You will have a basket?" he asked, mopping the groaning man's brow with a clean cloth.

"Yes, again." Mary Beth smiled, knowing what was coming.

"Would you mind if I were to bid?"

"Why Doctor Gil—"

"Tom," he corrected.

Mary Beth hesitated. "It's a benefit. The object is to raise money for the church. If you were to bid, it would mean just that much more for the church fund." She felt giddily shy as the young doctor turned to look at her.

"I'll be there. And I'll be the one who has supper with you."

Mary Beth laughed. Then turning serious she asked, "How long before I can take him home to Charley Good Book's?"

"I'll take him on over after I bind that arm. You go on, if you need to . . . Mary Beth." Again he flashed her a brilliant smile.

"Well, I do have a lot to do. Guess I'll see you tonight."

"Tonight." He walked Mary Beth to her buggy and helped her up. She waved at him as she reined away. He was certainly a handsome man. Mary Beth wondered why she didn't feel more of an attraction for him.

By the time she arrived home, the shadows from the two large sycamores in the front yard had almost reached the house. She handed the reins to Pedro and hurried inside. She was sure her father was home because someone had tracked the flour she'd spilled across the kitchen floor. She yelled for her father, then wondered when he didn't answer. She walked to the stairway.

"Father!" she called out. There was no answer.

"Nels Nelson, you tracked flour all over my floors!" She glanced down. The powdery white footprints continued up the stairs.

Returning to the kitchen, Mary Beth donned a clean apron, stoked up the fire in the cast-iron cook stove, then quickly cleaned up the mess. The lard could not be used for a pie crust now, so she spooned some into a skillet, and quickly prepared her Aunt Gus's favorite blend of flour and spices. Next she cut up and rolled a chicken in the mixture and began frying it. When she picked up the bowl of berries and walked to the cooler, she noticed there were not enough left for a pie. That was strange.

Mary Beth checked the kitchen wall clock. She'd have to hurry. She had just enough time to lay her clothes out before turning the chicken. Reaching the head of the stairs, she again called out to her father. There was still no answer. A cold chill swept down her spine.

Maybe her father was not the one who had tracked the flour. It was not like him.

Mary Beth hesitated, then decided she was just being silly. Her father was probably out in the carriage house. She went on up to her room.

One of the drawers in her bureau was pulled out slightly, and a pair of lace undergarments was draped over the edge. A small drawer on the dressing table had been removed completely and was sitting on the table top.

Mary Beth's heart began to pound.

The door to her tiny dressing area was ajar.

She thought of running from the room, but instead walked slowly to the door and peeked through the crack. Then she flung the door open wide.

Except for the many bustled gowns which lined the walls, the room was empty.

Mary Beth jumped as she heard the front door slam. Then her father called out to her. Remembering the chicken, she scampered back down the stairs.

CHAPTER EIGHTEEN

Getting duded up was not one of Ned Cody's favorite pastimes. His only suit had been pressed and laid out on the bed of his hotel room. He shined his boots and dressed, then digging into a bureau drawer, he found the old sock that held his savings. Ned shook the coins and a few paper dollars out onto the bed and counted. There was only a little over eighteen dollars, but his scrip from the City for the month of June was overdue. Pocketing five dollars, he returned the rest to the sock and placed it back in the drawer.

A box social was a fund-raiser for the Baptist church, which did not yet have its own building, conducting its services in the city meeting hall each Sunday morning. Ned was expected to attend since most of the City Council members were Baptists. Besides, Cody knew Mary Beth would be there.

He was actually looking forward to the whole thing. The objective was to outbid the other fellows so you could share your favorite lady's basket with her, to find out what kind of cook she was, if you didn't already know.

As he was pulling on his coat, Ned was startled by an explosion out in the street. He reached quickly for the .44 hanging on the bedpost. The first report was soon followed by the staccato blasts of more explosions. Ned recognized the noise as a string of firecrackers being set off. Someone was beginning to celebrate early.

He tried to decide whether or not to wear the large gun. It didn't look quite right under the suit coat. Instead he put his smaller .36 in his boot and carried the .44 in its holster and belt over his shoulder. He would leave it behind on the coat tree in his office.

The hall was full by the time Ned arrived. He searched the room until he saw Mary Beth. She looked radiant in a dress the color of spring lupines, her blond hair pulled straight back. To Ned, she seemed by far the prettiest woman in town and probably in the five surrounding counties. Mary Beth was engaged in an animated conversation with Doctor Gilroy and her father. Cody decided to wait until after the bidding, when he owned her basket, to chit-chat with her. Pouring himself a glass of punch, Cody walked over to a group of men discussing the upcoming special election.

"If ya' ask me, the Constitution of 1849 leaves a lot to be desired," one of the merchants argued. "It was written by a lot of fellows who knew little about government. We got to have another. We got to have one that takes all of us into consideration."

"Poppycock," the station master of the railroad office at Sumner commented. "The one we have now suits us and the rest of California just fine. It —"

"You mean it suits the railroads fine," the merchant said, interrupting. "And the banks and the big mining interests. Those boys in Sacramento don't even know we exist way down here. The politicians want to pull the same kind of shenanigans they pulled getting Rutherfraud B. Hayes elected. And it ain't gonna' work this time." The merchant referred to the President's recently acquired nickname. The recent election of Rutherford B. Hayes by the Electoral College had overridden the popular vote. Well over a year later, it was still a much-discussed and cussed issue.

"Well, I'm running for Delegate," the station manager said, raising his drink to the rest of the group. "I hope all you fellows will give me your vote."

"Vote for him and you're votin' for the railroads and the banks," the merchant snarled, keeping his glass lowered, "and the same kind of bull that got Ruther*fraud* elected over the will of the people."

The special elections for the California delegation to investigate changing the State's constitution were nearing and tempers were running high. The argument stopped when the Baptist minister crossed up to the podium. Motioning for everyone to stand, he uttered a preacher's normal long-winded blessing over the crowd. He got a chuckle when he prayed for "vigorous competition for the baskets."

Then he called on the ladies. "Please bring your baskets to the podium."

Mary Beth cast a sideways glance at Ned as she passed him, but coyly said nothing. Cody could never have mistaken the basket she was carrying. It was covered with a lace cloth and tied with a bright purple ribbon that matched her gown.

Four baskets were bid on quickly, the highest price paid being two dollars and a quarter — two day's wages for a cowhand or a Deputy Marshal, and more than a day's pay for a City Marshal. Cody stepped forward when the minister reached for Mary Beth's basket.

Before Cody had the chance to speak, Nels Nelson had bid a dollar, and Doc Gilroy upped it to two. Mary Beth smiled demurely at Ned as he raised his hand and shouted, "Two and a half." A couple of other fellows had just raised their hands when a firm hand grabbed Cody's shoulder.

Ned stared at the barber who jabbered at him excitedly. "You got some trouble over at Callahan's, Marshal. Ratzlaff ask me to tell you. He was hightailing it that way."

Reluctantly, Ned headed for his office. Grabbing the .44 off the coat rack, he strapped it on while his long strides carried him out the door and into the street.

It was two blocks at a trot to the Oyster and Chop House. Callahan's was packed with cowhands and miners who had come to town for the celebration. They were jammed against the swinging doors and Ned had to shove his way inside. The back half of Callahan's was almost empty.

It didn't take a moment to see what the trouble was.

Theo Ratzlaff stood with his hands on his hips, talking to Toothless Gum San Choy, who had a very frightened Mexican pinned in the corner. Gum San had a hatchet raised over the terrified man's head. The Mexican was cowering on his knees, pleading with the little wizened Chinaman not to split his skull.

Toothless rattled threateningly in Chinese.

"Now come on, Toothless," Ratzlaff said quietly, "we can handle this. Let me take him in and you can bring Ling Su to take a look at him." Theo took a step forward and Toothless raised the hatchet a little higher, shaking his head emphatically.

Ned stepped in between Theo and the irate Chinaman. "Honorable friend of my father," Cody said quietly.

Toothless lowered the hatchet a bit bowing almost imperceptibly. "This look like man daughter say steal hens, Marsh' Ned. I chop off head an' take to her." The Mexican shrunk even lower into the corner.

"Now, Toothless. That's not the way we're gonna do it. Let me take a look at him." Ned walked forward, and Toothless lowered the hatchet completely. The Mexican almost fell prostrate into the corner.

Ned lifted the man's chin, looking for the telltale scar described on the Tenkiller poster. It was true that the frightened man resembled the murderous half-breed, but there was no hangman's scar.

"This is not the man I spoke of, Tooth-less," Cody said to his friends. "Still, he does look like the one Ling Su described. I'll take him over to the jail and you bring your daughter to take a look at him."

"I get her now," Toothless replied, running towards the front door, excitedly. The crowd gave him plenty of room, falling over themselves to get out of the way as he passed. The hatchet swinging from his hand was almost brushing the floor.

Ned laughed and extended his hand to the Mexican, helping him to his feet. "You almost lost your smile there, friend," the Marshal said. The man clambered up, knocking a chair aside, shaking his head.

Theo walked over to Ned. "I was walkin' down Chester," Ratzlaff explained, chuckling, "just watching to make sure no one was raisin' too much hell. And I saw this fella makin' tracks for Callahan's. Toothless was right on his heels swingin' that ax like he was tryin' to fell a redwood an' screamin' that Chinee gibberish at the top of his lungs."

"Well, I'm glad you got here, Theo. Toothless has been a little upset lately."

"Upset?" the Mexican cried. He walked to the bar, picked up the first glass of whiskey he came to, and downed it. Turning back to the lawmen, he said, "If that was 'upset', *Señor,* I would not care to see mad."

Ned motioned the man to the door. "You're still gonna have to come back to the office and wait 'til he brings his daughter."

"Awww, Marshal!" The Mexican gave Ned an exasperated look, then turned to Jimmy "One Eye" Callahan. The saloon keeper stood leaning against the back bar with Betsy cradled in the crook of his arm.

"Gimme three fingers of Who Hit John," the Mexican ordered, slapping a coin down on the bar. Jimmy smiled, returning Betsy under the bar, and poured the customer five fingers. The still-shaking Mexican downed it without a breath, then followed the two lawmen out.

The Mexican tucked himself protectively between the lawmen, mumbling, "If that skinny yellow sombitch is coming back, you fellows can lock me up."

By the time Toothless arrived, with a very apprehensive Ling Su in tow, Ned had already inspected the man's boot heel and found no corresponding nick.

Ling Su stared carefully at the man, whose hair was neatly trimmed, not long and stringy like that of her attacker. She studied his pleading eyes for a moment, then shook her head. Ratzlaff returned the frightened Mexican to the streets.

Ned gave Toothless a short, obligatory lecture about taking the law into his own hands, then hurried back into the crowded meeting hall.

By now everyone was seated and eating. Ned walked over to where Doc Gilroy, Nels, and Mary Beth were finishing off plates of fried chicken and potato salad, and were about to start on bowls of berries and cream.

"Congratulations, Doc. You got the prettiest basket and the prettiest girl at the party." Ned's regret was obvious from the tone of his voice.

"And the best cook, if I'm any judge." The doctor looked at Mary Beth and smiled. "And I am."

Mary Beth looked up coolly from pouring cream on the berries. "I'd offer you some chicken, Marshal Cody, but it cost Tom seven dollars." She returned to her serving.

Neither the "Marshal Cody" nor the "Tom" was lost on Ned and he winced noticeably. He only had five dollars on him and he would have lost the bidding anyway.

"He was already kind enough to share

254

with me, Marshal," Nels Nelson added smugly, then noticed the gun belt. "This is hardly the place to be wearin' that gun, young man!"

"You're right, Mr. Nelson. Guess I'd better get back out on the street." As he walked to the door, Ned fully expected Mary Beth to call him back with an excuse for not accompanying him to the picnic tomorrow. But she didn't. Nor did she say good night. As Ned shut the door behind him, a fiddle and guitar squeaked and strummed out a reel.

Ned spent the rest of Friday night helping Ratzlaff patrol the streets and making sure the sound of exploding fireworks was no more than that.

CHAPTER NINETEEN

Saturday was hotter than a bull in a heifer pen. And Ned was sure it would be at least as much trouble.

The firecrackers had begun cracking and booming even before the stores opened. A couple of schoolboys sent Whiskey Lem skipping down Chester Avenue, hitting the street about every third step, slapping at the string of firecrackers they'd stuffed into his rear pocket. Luckily, he wore long johns even in the summer heat and had some extra padding, so nothing was really hurt, except what little pride he still had left.

Streamers and bunting flapped in the breeze. A new American flag hung from a rope that crossed the main intersection of Nineteenth and Chester. It was the first thing Ned noticed when he looked out the window of his room at sun up. The city crew had done a good job decorating, and Ned's chest swelled with pride as he watched the big American flag wave in what little breeze the morning offered. The crew had left oil lights glowing brightly on all four corners of Nineteenth and Chester all night long, so the flag would be properly lit.

A group of fellows who called themselves "the Empire Club" were in town for the picnic's big event: a baseball game. Ned had never seen it played, except for when the Bakersfield team, "the Two Orphans," practiced at the city park. There had never been a real game in town. Ned had trouble believing the Empire Club would be able to see the ball when they awoke. They'd raised hell half the night until the hotel management got Ned out of bed to quiet them down. They had been so drunk that Cody had to help three of them find their rooms in the middle of the night.

Ned himself had not had a good night's sleep.

As he made his way to the office, Ned thought about his problems with Sheriff George Howard. Cody hadn't seen Howard nor any of his boys around town last night. Ned didn't really believe that his run-in with the county law would keep them out of the city, nor prevent them from continuing their protection-for-pay activities.

Still, they must be lying low for some

reason. Ned wondered why.

The city stayed relatively quiet for the rest of the morning. Everyone must be saving up for the afternoon, Ned reckoned, and for the big fireworks planned for that night.

At eleven he returned to his hotel room and changed into a clean shirt. Cody dreaded his ride out to the big yellow house, half expecting Mary Beth to bow out, claiming sickness or something when he got to her door. But she didn't. She bounced happily down the stairs, responding to her father's call.

"You're right on time, Marshal Cody," she said, smiling.

"Ned, remember? We agreed. You look lovely, Miss Nelson."

"Why thank you, sir. Are we ready to go picnicking?" She flashed Ned a brilliant smile. After much soul-searching, Mary Beth had decided that she'd acted silly towards him the night before. After all, she had had no date with Ned Cody. She'd simply hoped he would bid on her basket, which he did. He'd bid more than any other basket had sold for, in fact, right up until he left.

Besides, she had had a grand time talking with Tom Gilroy, who'd set the record for the church social by paying seven dollars for her basket. He was a charming, educated man. And a very good-looking one. Still, he seemed almost too nice.

She wondered what lawman's business had taken Cody away in such a hurry. It was just the kind of thing she hated most about men with badges.

Her morning had gone perfectly, until she started looking for the brooch she usually wore with her blue gingham dress. The brooch featured a large amethyst surrounded with pearls in a gold setting and had been left to her by her mother. Mary Beth loved it, but now it was missing. She was sure it had been in the drawer table. When she mentioned it to her father, Nels stomped around angrily, raving about the help and how you could trust no one these days. Mary Beth tried to calm him down, assuring her father that she had probably just misplaced it, and begging him not to fire anyone until she had a chance to search further. But Mary Beth knew someone had been in her room.

Carrying the picnic basket that she'd worked on all morning, Ned helped Mary Beth into the carriage he'd borrowed from old Mr. McGillicutty. "Would your father like to come along with us, Mary Beth?" Ned asked politely, hoping otherwise.

"No. He may join us later. I understand the baseball game starts right at noon, but Papa thinks that it's all a bunch of foolishness." She laughed and Cody grinned. Then Ned whipped up the mare and they headed off into town.

"Should be interesting to watch," Ned said. "The team our boys are s'posed to play stayed at the Southern last night. I kinda wonder if there's gonna be a game at all. Those boys were sure in their cups." The small talk continued until they pulled up at the city park. First they staked out a spot to spread out the cloth Mary Beth had packed, and parked the basket. Then they walked over to the playing field.

As they strolled along, she mentioned the missing brooch and the possibility of an intruder. Ned's jaw tightened for a moment as his mind flashed on what Tenkiller had done to Ling Su. Next time it could be Mary Beth. The vision was followed by a twinge of guilt that Cody was here and not out on the streets searching. But then Mary Beth changed the subject and Ned was lost in her smile and flashing blue eyes.

Al Cuen was sick.

He'd awakened and had to push Chapa out of the way as he scrambled outside and threw up. All Friday he'd alternated between spells of dizziness and up-chucking. Now his head ached terribly.

Tia Carlita kept trying to force food on him. To the fat madam, food was the ultimate cure-all. But try as he may, Cuen just couldn't keep it down.

On Saturday morning, Tia Carlita was sitting at Al's bedside when he awoke. He tried to sit up, but grabbed his throbbing head and dropped back to the bed.

"I have the girls cooking you a fine breakfast, Don Alvarado," Carlita said, reaching over and patting his shoulder. "It looks like you will want it in bed." She tried to speak happily, but the concern in her voice was obvious.

"I don't think I can hold a thing down, Tia," Al replied, his voice little more than a whisper. "My head is still terrible."

"I think I take you to the doctor today. You have been hit much too hard. I think he broke your *cabeza,* Don Alvarado. I will get the wagon."

"No, Tia. You will not haul me to town like a load of manure. I will rest here. I will be fine." He waved her away.

"I will be back when the food is prepared." Tia Carlita started to leave, but paused and looked back with concern. Then she closed the door behind her.

"This has to be done just right, *mi amigos.*" George Howard leaned forward in his swivel chair, elbows on his knees, and instructed the Urrea brothers.

The Mexicans stood and started for the door. Then Ricardo turned back. "The horses and the money, at three o'clock?"

"Like I said, *amigos.* Three o'clock. Eighteen shiny fifty-dollar gold pieces."

Enrico looked suspiciously at the Sheriff. "Are you sure you do not want Tenkiller dead? I think it would be a very easy thing."

"You boys do this just as I told you. I got my reasons." George Howard stood and walked them to the door. Before opening it, he added, "You boys will be livin' high on the hog in Hermosillo. High on the hog."

After the Mexican brothers had left, Howard motioned Puttyworth and Winston into his office.

"You boys ready?" Howard asked.

"You sure we shouldn't have Big Jim Jackson here, Sheriff?" Puttyworth offered.

"No. I told you boys, I want only my most trusted deputies in on this." Both deputies smiled at the compliment. "Besides," Howard continued, "it's too late to try an' get him down here. You boys just do as I say and everything is gonna go like clockwork."

The two deputies walked to the rack of long guns that lined one full wall of George Howard's office. Puttyworth took down a scattergun, then filled his pocket with shells. Winston grabbed a 73 Winchester and a handful of cartridges. Together they walked purposefully out into the sweltering July day.

"I tol' you, *novio mi,* the other girls will be along soon," said one Urrea sister, stroking Tenkiller's brow. He pushed her hand away. He hated women fawning over him.

Johnny Tenkiller lay back on the bed and relaxed. Ricardo had told him about two of the most beautiful crib girls in the city, and had promised to have them there that afternoon. A beautiful, long-legged blonde and a mulatto from New Orleans who spoke French while she did things that only French mulattos knew how to do.

It should be worth the wait, Johnny thought. A final taste of the Bakersfield girls before he left. The brothers did not know it, but tonight Tenkiller planned to visit Cordova's bar at closing time and relieve the saloon owner of his daily profits. Then it was back to Arizona. Or perhaps Pueblo Los Angeles. Johnny had never been there before.

The Urrea sisters had strict instructions to keep Tenkiller well-occupied until their brothers' return. Then they were to get as far away from Charley Good Book's as they could. They did not ask why, but they knew their brothers. Far away it would be.

The girls heard steps on the stairway and peered out. Toothless Gum San Choy bowed his head to them as he walked crab-like down the narrow hallway. Heavy clay crocks hung on straps from a carrying stick that rested across his bony shoulders. Toothless sidestepped to the room of the Chinese lady and softly knocked. The Urrea sisters smiled knowingly to each other and closed the door.

Johnny Tenkiller stood and stretched. Then he sat back down and started to pull on his boots.

One of the girls moved quickly to the bed and curled around him. "Johnny," she said in her sexiest voice, "we are jealous. You will have the company of two beautiful women this afternoon. Do you not care for us?" The girl feigned a pout.

"Of course," Johnny said, coming as close to smiling as the sisters had seen since his arrival. "But now I want a bottle of whiskey." He reached down and continued pulling on a boot.

The other girl jumped forward. "I have money, Johnny," she said, excitedly. "Let me get it for you?" She turned and scampered for the door. Johnny hesitated, then shrugged his shoulders and lay back on the bed.

As the girl descended the stairs, she met her brothers coming up. "I thought I told you to stay with him," Ricardo chastised her.

"He was going out to get whiskey. I told him I would go."

Ricardo nodded his head thoughtfully. "You did well, little sister. Now go quickly, and bring the bottle back. Then I want you to take your sister far away."

"Be careful, my brothers, whatever it is you do." The girl hurried down the steps and out into the street.

Ricardo and Enrico gave the signal knock that Johnny insisted upon, then shoved the door open. "The girls will be here soon, Johnny," Ricardo told him through the closed connecting door.

Tenkiller stayed in the sisters' room, while Ricardo and Enrico rolled cigarettes and smoked. The brothers waited impatiently for three o'clock.

The baseball game was over. The Two

Orphans team had beaten the Empire Club 31 to 6. There'd been only one fist fight when the opposing pitcher did not pitch slow enough so the Two Orphans team could easily hit the ball, as the rules said he must. But Ned Cody was content to leave the altercation up to the umpire.

Now it was time to eat, and Ned was happy to note that Nels Nelson still had not shown up. Maybe Ned would have Mary Beth all to himself.

They spread the cloth, and Ned walked to a stand were a vendor was selling a unique July product — ice. The vendor had hauled it down from high up in the Sierras. It would cool the small crock of buttermilk Mary Beth had packed.

Mary Beth had been wonderful company and Ned Cody couldn't help but wish they were completely alone. Perhaps in a meadow in the cool, high mountains, instead of struggling for shade in the crowded city park.

As Mary Beth unpacked the basket, Ned's mouth began to water. She'd prepared the same delicious-looking fried chicken Cody had seen the night before, plus a green salad, a fruit salad, and a potato salad. The meal was rounded out with fresh baked bread, and the prettiest golden-crusted pie

Ned had ever seen. Still he could not resist a little tease as she loaded his plate.

"Leftovers?"

"Why, Ned Cody! I'll have you know I was up with the sun, frying that chicken and baking this pie."

"Whoa! I was just kidding. It looks delicious."

Just as she handed Cody the heaping plate, Cap Colston came running up behind them.

"Cody," the deputy said, panting and wheezing, "you gotta' come right now! John Tenkiller!" Colston stopped for a moment, puffing for breath.

Cody got to his feet.

"John Tenkiller is at Charley Good Book's boardinghouse. Been staying there with the Urrea brothers."

"Where's the Sheriff and his boys?" Ned asked.

Colston cut his eyes away. "Don't know. Couldn't find them anywhere."

Cody paused, glancing back at Mary Beth. She rose to her feet, her surprised look turning to one of disgust, then hurt.

"I'm sorry Mary Beth," Ned apologized. "I gotta go."

"Ned Cody, if you leave me don't you ever —" But Cody was already gone, moving at

267

a dead run to where he'd left the buggy tied.

Cap Colston stared at the spread on the ground and then at Mary Beth. "If the Marshal doesn't have time to eat that, I wouldn't mind —"

Mary Beth spun on her heels and stomped away.

Al Cuen was going through a particularly bad spell. Beads of sweat covered his forehead and his head pounded as if a blacksmith was fitting it for horseshoes.

Tia Carlita pushed open the door carrying a big tray of food. "Here, Don Alvarado," she said, "this will make you feel better." She sat the tray down, noticing the fitful look in Alvarado's eyes and the sweat on his brow. "No more arguments, Al Cuen," she told him emphatically. "You are going to the doctor."

Carlita left, but returned a few moments later. Helping Cuen to his feet, she led him to the front of the *hacienda* where a wagon waited. "Get in the back," the fat woman ordered. She had thrown a pillow into the bed of the small buckboard wagon.

"No, Tia," Cuen protested weakly, "I'll not ride like a load of manure. I told you."

"No one will see you, Alvarado. You will be inside the wagon. I will drive you myself."

"No! No! Get my horse. I'll go, but only on my horse." He sat on the porch, then lay his head down on the cool bricks and waited.

"Your head was not so hard when the gringo hit you. Why is it so hard now?" Tia Carlita complained, but nonetheless motioned a boy to fetch Alvarado's horse.

Calling for a wet towel, she had Chapa sit next to Cuen to wipe his brow as they waited. The boy came with the horse, and by then Al was feeling a little better. Tia Carlita supported him as he lifted a foot into the stirrup. But dizziness overtook him as he tried to mount and Cuen stumbled back into the big woman's arms. "Bring the wagon," she instructed the boy, who brought it close and dropped the tailgate.

Alvarado did not argue about the wagon now. "Tie the horse to the rear of the wagon, *muchacho,*" Al said weakly as he crawled between the two foot-high sideboards. He laid his head on the pillow and felt like retching again.

The boy and Chapa helped Tia Carlita mount the wagon. Chapa balanced her and the boy pushed from behind, both hands almost disappearing beneath her massive buttocks. Chapa insisted on going too, so she climbed into the back and sat beside

Don Alvarado Cuen, who kept his eyes quietly shut as the wagon bumped over the rough road, the big stallion trailing behind.

Ned Cody saw Ratzlaff on the street as he raced the buggy to the office. He reined up and slowed enough for Theo to scramble aboard.

"What's up," the big deputy shouted over the noise of the galloping horse and rattling buggy.

"John Tenkiller. He's at Charley Good Book's. I should have known." Ned stared intently at the road in front of them. "I remembered after I left the picnic. The tin box Max used to keep his money in was on the dresser in the Urreas' room at Charley's, but I didn't recognize it. It didn't have any money in it. It was full of the gumdrops Max always gave the kids."

"You gonna get some county help?"

"Colston was the one that tol' me Tenkiller was there. He said he couldn't find any of his own people."

Ratzlaff smiled slightly. "Probably just as well." They careened around the corner onto Chester Avenue. The street was crowded, and people on foot and horseback scattered frantically out of their way. "Me knocking Winston over the bar," Theo

270

continued, "and you feeding your gun barrel to Puttyworth . . . we'd be havin' to watch our backs more 'n watching out for the half-breed."

Before the buggy reached a full stop, they jumped down and ran into the office. Ned grabbed the old Parker scattergun from its pegs while Ratzlaff dug into a desk drawer for more cartridges for his .44. Ned strapped on his own .44, then shoved the .36 in his boot. Hesitating only a moment, he took a deep breath and looked at his deputy. "You ready?" Cody asked.

Ratzlaff slapped him on the back. "This should be about as much fun as gettin' hung with a new rope."

They didn't gallop the buggy as they headed for Charley Good Book's. They walked the horse slowly, carefully planning their arrest.

"I'll drop you off down the street, Theo," Cody began, his expression hard and serious. "You head across the back yards and go in the rear way. The Urreas' rooms — they got two — are on the south side, on the second floor near the middle. Rooms twenty-two and twenty-four.

"I'll pass in the buggy, then drop off an' head in the front door. We'll meet on the second floor. You take the back stairs. I'll take the front."

"What about the Urrea boys?" Ratzlaff interrupted. "You think they'll get in the way?"

"If they do, it'll be three to two."

"Well, we ought to have the advantage of surprise, and that's worth two Mexicans or Chinamen any day." Ratzlaff laughed nervously. Then he jumped, startled, as a boy set off a string of firecrackers nearby.

Johnny Tenkiller sat on the bed drinking whiskey from the bottle. He eyed Ricardo suspiciously. The man had looked at his pocket watch ten times in the last few minutes, while Enrico had "walked to the front to watch for the girls."

"Why are you so nervous, *amigo*?" Johnny asked the pacing Ricardo.

"I promised you the girls would be here at three, Johnny . . . an' something else —"

"What?" Tenkiller got to his feet.

"I heard something. Just a rumor, I'm sure."

"What rumor?"

"I heard on the street this morning that the gringo Marshal — Cody — I heard he was looking for you. Looking very hard."

Johnny's face relaxed as he sat back on the bed. "So what, *amigo*? The law has been looking for me 'very hard' for as long as I can remember."

The sound of running footsteps echoed on the other side of the door. A quick code knock followed.

Tenkiller uncocked the stubby revolver that he had palmed and leveled it at the door, just as Enrico stuck his head in. "They come! The city Marshal and the deputy! In a buggy!"

Johnny was on his feet instantly, the .450 in one hand and the Henry in the other. "The tunnel," he mumbled, starting for the door.

"No, Johnny," Ricardo said, stepping in front of him. "There is not time. Enrico and I will help you. We get the Marshal first. Then the tunnel."

John Tenkiller looked from Ricardo to his brother with surprise. They seemed determined. Maybe he'd misjudged them.

"*Bueno.* Then we can take our time." Johnny smiled a yellow-toothed grin, thinking that he would still be able to pay a visit to Cordova and his money box, if the Marshal was lying face down in the street.

"Johnny, you go with Enrico to the front," Ricardo instructed. "I'll take the back of the house." The Urreas had spent hours planning just how they would greet Marshal

Ned Cody and his deputy, if Cody brought him along.

Reaching the stairs, Enrico turned to Tenkiller. "I'll take the roof over the porch," Urrea said. "You take the front door."

Enrico began tugging at the window at the end of the hall, the only access to the porch roof. Johnny hesitated a moment, then decided that the roof was a very good place for the Henry rifle. Enrico carried the shotgun and a belly gun. Neither was worth a damn at more than twenty-five paces.

Enrico looked up in surprise when Johnny followed him onto the roof, but said nothing.

They immediately dropped to all fours and crawled to the false railing that rimmed the porch roof. From there, they could see the buggy in the intersection at the end of the block. The large deputy waited as Cody walked the buggy toward the joss house. Then Ratzlaff hurried out of sight down the side street.

"Let him get very close," Tenkiller whispered.

Al Cuen was feeling a little better by the time he was able to recognize the rooftops of Bakersfield from his reclining position in the back of the buckboard. Chapa had been tenderly wiping his brow as they bumped along, and his mind was off his aching head, and on the full bosom that hung temptingly near his face.

He watched curiously, noticing two men armed with long guns on the porch roof of Charley Good Book's. One of them looked like the bartender from Cordova's. The buckboard plodded on.

"*Buenos dias,* Marshal," Tia Carlita said to an unseen passing buggy.

Al sat up quickly.

Fighting dizziness, he stumbled to his feet. He sprang from the back of the buckboard into the saddle of the trailing horse. Though both women were yelling at him, Al Cuen could not hear a single word.

He reached for the whip at his back, only to realize that he'd left it behind in the room at Tia Carlita's.

Spurring the horse, spinning and retracing the wagon's tracks, Al Cuen had his sixty-foot *reata* in his hands by the time he galloped past Cody in the buggy. "Watch out!" Al screamed as he sped by the surprised Marshal.

Ricardo, watching out the back door of the house, decided all the action was going to be at the front. He crept down the back porch stairs, a brand-new 73 Winchester in

his hand courtesy of Sheriff George Howard, and made his way through the crates
and boxes toward the front of the joss house.

Creeping to within twenty feet of the
front, Ricardo saw Alvarado gallop by. The
long loop of Cuen's *reata* flicked out toward
the porch roof and dropped securely over
the corner post. Al took a dally on his saddle
horn and spurred the big black stallion.

Tenkiller had raised up to get a bead on
Ned Cody's chest, just as Ned realized what
Cuen was up to. Cody whipped the mare
and the buggy leaped forward. He heard
the report of the Henry, and saw a belch of
flame on the porch roof. Cody felt the hot
slug crease the back of his right shoulder.

Enrico leaned over the railing and took a
bead on the retreating Mexican as Tenkiller
levered another shell into the Henry.

Ratzlaff abandoned the idea of using the
back door and jumped the rear fence into
the yard of the joss house. Then he heard
the report of Tenkiller's rifle. As Ratzlaff ran
to the front to help Cody, Ricardo dived
behind one of the crates cluttering the side
yard.

Atop the porch roof, Enrico realized it was
Don Alvarado Cuen whom he had in his
sights, but that was fine by him. He
squeezed the trigger just as Cuen's *reata*

tightened. The big stallion's full weight pulled against the well-woven leather *reata,* and the lassoed post was ripped from the porch roof.

Suddenly, the entire corner of the porch roof collapsed.

Al Cuen's head swam with dizziness as he tumbled from the saddle into the dust, and passed out.

Cody dove from the buggy into the street and rolled. His scattergun rode away with the departing horse and buggy while he scrambled for cover behind one of Charley Good Book's carved gate dogs.

Enrico's shotgun blast went wild as he tumbled from the collapsing roof. Tenkiller landed on top of him heavily, then scrambled to his feet and ran to the front door. The roof was now angling down from the second floor to the ground. Tenkiller kicked open the front door of the joss house and rolled inside.

Ned ducked around the side of a gate dog, his .44 cocked and ready. He could just make out the legs of the prostrate form of a man, and the barrel of a shotgun, through cracks between the barrels and crates.

Enrico saw Ratzlaff running across the side yard. The Mexican quickly swung the shotgun up and took aim. Ned felt the panic in Theo's eyes and fired the big .44 into the knee of the prostrate form holding the shotgun. But Cody's shot was a second too late, finding its mark at the same instant Enrico's scattergun roared out its second deadly boom. Theo Ratzlaff was blown backwards into the dirt.

Ned's shot rang true. He saw Enrico's leg snap, then jerk out of sight.

Ned waited.

Ricardo Urrea had always disliked Theodore Ratzlaff and he now saw his chance to finish off the big deputy. The Mexican rose from his hiding place and cocked the Winchester.

Ratzlaff's .44 had been flung out of reach by the shotgun blast. He couldn't have used it anyway. Clutching his mangled, blood-soaked right shoulder with his left hand, Theo awaited his fate. The clicking of the Winchester's hammer reverberated down Theo's spine as he stared into the hollow, merciless eye of the rifle.

Ricardo took a bead on the big deputy just as the window on the second floor above him swung open.

Toothless had been watching from Gi Lu's window, wishing he had his hatchet. Gi Lu wanted nothing to do with any of it and scampered for the door.

Toothless grabbed the only weapon at hand. He flung the heavy crock full of eggs and pickling liquid down onto Ricardo's head, eight feet below.

The 73 went off, deafening the wide-eyed Theo Ratzlaff, the slug burying itself harmlessly in the dirt just inches beside his face.

His skull crushed, his neck broken, Ricardo slammed into the dirt. His last thought was of Hermosillo, the city he would never see.

Theo's fleeting thought, just before he passed out, was, "God bless Chinamen."

Ned could wait no longer. He dived from behind the carved gate dog and rolled into the front yard, banging into a pile of empty crates. Holstering his .44, Cody took a step back and charged the cluttered boxes and barrels that separated him from the man with the shotgun. They tumbled and crashed noisily. Rolling to his side, Ned again palmed his .44. The bartender from Cordova's struggled to his feet, one hand clutching his bloodied knee, the other pawing at his belly as he grappled for a hidden gun.

"Don't do it!" Ned shouted. Ignoring him, Enrico palmed a wicked little Derringer.

Ned fired, and the .44 slug took the man in the middle of the chest, blowing him backwards.

The bartender twitched twice, then stilled.

Carefully, Ned peered into the darkness where the collapsed porch leaned against the front of the joss house. The front door to Charley's was open. "Hope you're on our side," Ned mumbled at the crucified Jesus. Cody hesitated, then charged inside.

Keeping his back flat against the wall, Ned inched down the long hallway toward the rear stairway. He passed a door, and almost fell into it as it opened suddenly. Cody spun and dropped to the floor. A surprised Chinaman Ned had never seen before stared into the barrel of Cody's .44. The man slammed the door and Ned rose to his feet, glad that Hiram had told him the story about the wild shooting in Visalia. He could have mistakenly sent the man to wherever Chinese go when their time on earth ends.

He heard footsteps coming down the rear stairway. Gi Lu stopped on the stairs and stared at him.

She pointed over the railing to a stairway continuing down into the cellar.

"Man go to heavenly pleasures," she said. Then she turned and scrambled back upstairs.

I hope I can send him to hell's pleasures, Ned thought, descending the stairway into the dark cellar.

When he reached the bottom, he found the door that housed the Buddha was tightly shut. Ned kicked it open and several Chinese scrambled to the far wall.

Cody moved to the second door. He heard a crashing sound coming from inside. He kicked the door open and dropped to his knee in the same motion.

Fire spat from a gun muzzle deep inside the dark room.

Ned hit the floor and brought his left hand to the crease on his cheek. He felt the burn and the warm wetness of blood. But at least his head was still there.

Hearing what he thought was sloshing water, he rolled into the darkened room.

Nothing.

When Cody's eyes began to adjust to the dim light, he inched across the floor to an opening in the far wall of the storeroom. He could hear the sounds of a running man, sloshing through water, echoing in the distance.

Ned stepped back and dove into the small opening.

The muddy floor was two inches deep in water. Ned rose to his feet, pressing himself against the dirt wall. He was surprised he could stand up straight in the dark, confining void. Ned had heard many stories of the

tunnels the Chinese had under the Tenderloin, but had thought they were just so
much bull. Suddenly he had become a be-
liever.

Hearing another sound in the distance, he
slowly moved forward, with one hand extended to the side wall and the other holding the .44 out in front of him. Hearing the
distant footsteps abruptly stop, Ned froze,
and listened.

A second explosion of noise and fire
leaped out at him, this time lighting up the
whole tunnel. The wind of the passing slug
slapped at Ned and again he landed in the
mud.

Silence.

The sloshing sound of footsteps
continued.

Sheriff George Howard and deputies Puttyworth and Winston looked at each other in
surprise as shots reverberated from behind
the piece of charred sheet metal covering
the end of the tunnel.

"God damn." Puttyworth shook his head
in amazement. "Those boys is still at it!"
He and Winston had patted the fat sheriff
on the back when the first sounds of gunfire
pierced the afternoon air. But now the carefully laid plan of Sheriff George Howard's

seemed to be going sour. Tenkiller and the Urrea boys were supposed to have taken care of Marshal Ned Cody and his deputy, if he had happened to tag along, in the street in front of Charley's. They shouldn't still be shooting it out in the tunnel.

Howard and his deputies would have been "forced" to capture the fleeing Tenkiller, if possible, and kill the Urreas as they attempted their getaway. And everything would have ended well. Tenkiller would be history, either fodder for a vote-getting trial or dead. Ned Cody would simply be dead.

It still could end well. "You boys hunker down," Howard cautioned his deputies. "Somebody will be coming out that tunnel real soon. And whoever it is, weigh 'em down with lead."

The cellar of the burned-out blacksmith's shop was laced with charred timbers and weeds that had grown up since the fire two years earlier. A small portion of the building still stood above the ground level. That's where the county law waited, hidden behind the still-standing upper half, their guns pointed at the tunnel entrance in the cellar below.

Johnny Tenkiller came to the sun-heated sheet of metal closing off the end of the tunnel. Light filtered through the cracks where the metal was wedged against the masonry walls of the cellar.

He stepped back, and kicked at the metal with all his might. As it bulged out, more light flooded into the tunnel.

Ned flung himself back against the wall when the sound of Tenkiller's kick echoed back towards him.

The sound reverberated a second time.

Ned thought he caught a glimpse of light ahead, but still could make out nothing. Moving on, he touched a timber with his hand and realized that the tunnel turned.

The instant he saw light flooding the tunnel a shock of gun blasts slapped at him and Ned once again dove for the mud floor.

Johnny Tenkiller gave one final kick to the metal sheet blocking his escape and it crashed to the charred floor with a loud clang. Instantly gun blasts tore into the tunnel opening. Johnny got off one reflex shot before he was blown back into the tunnel opening.

He felt a warm wetness covering his side, and the searing pain of fire, and knew he'd been hit. But seeing one of the deputies slide face-first into the cellar, Johnny smiled. His shot had caught the ill-fated lawman square in the eye.

Johnny recognized the threat from above

and dropped to his knees. Another lawman was standing a little too high above the remnant of the wall. Johnny could just make out the top of his felt hat.

Tenkiller aimed low at the board wall, but his guess proved right. An instant after his .450 slug tore through the charred board, Johnny heard a shriek and saw the man in the felt hat spin away to the side.

Sheriff Howard realized that everything was going wrong. Puttyworth lay at the bottom of the cellar, the back of his head blown away. And Winston was pumping foaming lung blood from a gaping hole in his back as he laid face down mere inches from the trembling sheriff. Howard started to stand to hightail it to safety, just as Tenkiller stepped out of the tunnel.

A perfect silhouette for Ned Cody.

A huge .44 slug tore through John Tenkiller's upper chest, blowing him out onto the cellar floor. The stubby .450 was lost among the mud and charred lumber.

Howard stood and studied the prostrate figure of the killer lying below. Not a muscle twitched. The Sheriff began a slow descent down the cluttered stone stairway, his .44 in hand. Carefully, he watched John Tenkiller. The shot from the tunnel seemed to have done the job well.

Ned Cody sloshed the last fifty feet out into the light, and was surprised to see Sheriff Howard bending over Tenkiller.

"Where's Ratzlaff?" the sheriff asked.

"Got hit, before we even got inside," Ned answered, surprised at Howard's apparent concern. As Ned's eyes adjusted to the light, his gun hanging at his side, he was even more surprised to see Howard step forward and level his .44 at Cody's midsection.

"Drop that hog leg, Cody, you dumb peckerhead."

"What the hell are you doin', Howard?"

"Drop it!"

Ned did as he was told. His .44 splashed into the mud.

"I told you, you should have gone along, Cody," Howard hissed. "Now I'll have to break in a new marshal." As the big man talked, he bent over and searched through the muck for Tenkiller's stubby .450. Finding it, he motioned Ned back into the tunnel, palming Tenkiller's gun and stepping forward.

Ned saw John Tenkiller twitch behind Sheriff George Howard, and opened his mouth to warn the fat man.

"You keep your mouth shut, Cody," Howard snapped, "I'm holdin' all the cards now. All your 'city folks' will be real sad to find out old John Tenkiller was here and just a little bit faster than their peckerhead Marshal."

Tenkiller raised his head, slowly pulling himself to his knees as Sheriff Howard motioned Ned deeper into the tunnel.

Inching his way to his feet, Tenkiller took a deep breath and slipped a huge Bowie knife from its sheath into his palm. He stumbled, steadied himself again, then plunged forward. Howard heard a "smack" as one of Johnny's boots sucked out of the mud. He made a half turn, but an instant too late. Tenkiller was on him.

Howard's scream turned to gargle as the big knife sliced across his throat, cutting into his vocal cords and severing his jugular.

Howard fell to his knees, his hands feebly attempting to stop the bleeding. But the torrent of blood continued gushing from his throat, cascading through his grasping fingers.

John Tenkiller, now covered with his own blood and that of Sheriff George Howard, looked up locking gazes with Ned Cody.

Johnny smiled a half smile. "There will be no rope," he said. Screaming the war cry of his ancestors, Johnny charged forward, his knife raised, seeking one more throat before sheathing it for the last time.

Cody ducked just as Tenkiller reached him. The shrieking half-breed flew over him into the mud beyond. Ned stood, bringing the .36 out of his boot in just one fluid motion, as Tenkiller turned to launch himself again.

Ned shot the man between the eyes.

Tenkiller's bloodied face, and the gore-soaked Bowie knife, disappeared into the mud of the tunnel floor.

CHAPTER TWENTY

The lobby of the Southern Hotel and the small adjoining bar were packed with townspeople.

Theo Ratzlaff lay on a lobby sofa receiving the adulation of the crowd like a Czar. John Tenkiller, Ricardo Urrea, and Enrico Urrea were tied to flat boards and leaned up against the wall on the boardwalk of Chester Avenue, displayed like so many sides of beef. Their shirts had been removed and their wounds were the center of interest. Most of the talk was of who did what to whom.

Sheriff George Howard, Winston, and Puttyworth were in the rear room of Lightner's. The front of this establishment featured fine furniture of all kinds, and the rear the finest coffins. Lightner's served the customer both in here, and in the hereafter.

Ned Cody had not yet related the whole story to anyone. He'd decided he would wait until he spoke to the grand jury. Secretly he wondered if it wasn't best to let the dead rest in peace. There was nothing to be gained by smearing George Howard now. The man wouldn't be extorting any more money from the city's inhabitants.

Cody left the lobby and retreated to the quiet of his room. Doc Gilroy had patched the creases on his cheek and across his back, after he had taken care of Theo's more serious buckshot wounds. Theo was hurt badly, but he was as big and as tough as an ox. Even if his right shoulder didn't heal properly, he could learn to shoot left-handed. And Theo Ratzlaff could still whip most men with one hand.

Ned hoped to get away from the crowds by going to his room, but it was too full. More people came banging on his door every few seconds. He might as well have stayed in the lobby.

The one person he had really wanted to see hadn't shown. Cody guessed Mary Beth was so mad at him that it didn't matter how big a hero he was to the rest of the town. She had probably gone to join her stepmother in San Francisco.

Ned wanted to close his eyes for a few minutes, but his room was too full of men, all of them relating just where they'd been and what they'd been doin' when the biggest fireworks of the day had started.

To hell with it, Ned finally decided. He would head back to his office. Maybe there he could get a little peace and quiet. As he walked through the lobby, he paused to push through the crowd surrounding Theo Ratzlaff.

"Anything need doing at the office, Theo?"

Ratzlaff raised his head. "Not that I can think of, Ned. You goin' down there?"

"Yeah, I guess so. You need anything?" Ned laid a hand on the big man's good shoulder.

"Only one thing. If you see Toothless, I need to buy him a drink."

"And we both need to buy Al Cuen one," Ned said smiling. "How long does the Doc say you're gonna be laid up?"

"Well, I won't be joining the Two Orphans baseball team for a couple of months. But I'll be able to do desk work and watch the shop in a couple of weeks. At least if this shoulder doesn't fester."

Ned gave him a thumbs up, turned, and made his way out the front door. He paused a moment and looked through the crowd at the three dead men on their canted pedestals.

Toothless Gum San Choy stood beside

the bodies, his gums reflecting the sun as he smiled for the photographer. After the poof of the photographer's flash powder, he rubbed his eyes and walked over to Ned.

Ned grinned at the Chinaman. "Toothless, Theo said for me to tell you that he wanted to buy you a drink."

"No drink. Egg crock broken. Buy new egg crock."

"I know. Your very best egg crock." Ned smiled, then moved to the sallow body of John Tenkiller. Even in death, Tenkiller looked mean. Most other men would have been diminished by the display of their naked, bullet-ridden bodies. The raw-boned, sinuous frame of Tenkiller looked natural, like the most basic of predators.

As he walked on to his office, two young boys followed Cody, firing questions at him. He was saved when a buggy pulled up alongside. Hiram and his brother, Nels, waved Cody over.

Nels was the first to speak. "Just wanted to let you know, we appreciate the fact you kept that thing down in the Tenderloin, Ned."

"I didn't 'keep' it anywhere, Nels," Cody said. "I just tried to stop it as soon as I could." Ned resumed walking.

"You did a good job, Ned," Hiram said.

"Nobody on the street got hurt."

"Have you seen Al Cuen?" Ned decided that now was as good a time as any to broach the subject that was on his mind. "I'm gonna need another deputy an' I was thinkin' —".

"Hold on now, Cody," Nels interrupted. "Al Cuen's a Mexican."

Ned stopped in the street and turned to face Nels Nelson. "Alvarado Cuen's a Californian," he snapped, "and he saved my bacon. I'd be down in the back of Lightner's with those county boys if it wasn't for Cuen."

"Well, I don't know if we have the budget," Nels hedged.

Hiram patted his brother on the back. "You can make it happen, Nels. You always been able to do anything you set your mind to."

"But a Mex—"

"A Californian," Hiram corrected. "In fact, his folks were here when our daddy climbed off that clipper ship in New York . . . and had been for a hundred years, if I got my Cuens right."

Ned furrowed his brow. "Well, I guess we can figure some way," he mumbled.

Ned continued on towards the office.

As usual, someone was waiting at his office door. Mary Beth stood with her hands folded demurely in front of her, the picnic basket at her feet.

Hiram pulled the buggy up in front of the office, but made no effort to climb down. Harold Nels Nelson started to disembark, but Hiram whipped up the mare, almost dumping his brother out onto the ground. Nels managed to regain his seat. "I been wantin' to show you how well my orchard's doin'," Hiram said to his brother, as the buggy moved off at a trot.

Ned looked into Mary Beth's deep blue eyes.

"You all right?" she said reaching up and touching the patch on his cheek. "I would have come to the hotel to find you . . . but there were so many people."

"I'm hungry," Ned announced, smiling and eyeing the basket. "But first I've got something for you." He reached into his shirt pocket and dangled a brooch in front of her eyes. "Found this in Tenkiller's pocket. Is it yours?"

Cody could see the shocked recognition in her eyes. It was enough of an answer.

As they stepped into the office, Ned drew her in behind him and set the basket on his desk. Pulling her to him, Cody slipped an

arm around Mary Beth's waist, and quietly
pushed the door shut behind her.

ABOUT THE AUTHOR

L. J. Martin is the acclaimed, award-winning author of over 40 novels and non-fiction books. He was raised in the deserts of California and wrangled and packed horses throughout the Sierra, and later rode and hunted Montana, where he now lives with his wife, NYT bestselling romantic suspense and historical romance author Kat Martin. L. J. was in real estate development for much of his life, selling over one hundred million dollars in transactions the last year he worked in the field. He's traveled the world over, sailed his own ketch, been car wrecked, plane wrecked, beat, and bent . . . and dealt with some of the most powerful companies in the country. He knows the boardrooms and the backrooms of America, and her deep forests and wild high country. In wilder times he was the guest of many a *jusgados* but that's another story for another day. The Martins winter in California when not travelling for research on their novels.

We hope you have enjoyed this Large Print book. All our Thorndike, Wheeler, and Kennebec Large Print titles are designed for easy reading, and all our books are made to last. Other Thorndike Press Large Print books are available at your library, through selected bookstores, or directly from us.

For information about titles, please call:
(800) 223-1244

or visit our website at:
gale.com/thorndike

To share your comments, please write:
Publisher
Thorndike Press
10 Water St., Suite 310
Waterville, ME 04901